Tales of the Traveling Temptress

"A" Enjoy!

Love,
Lily

"Published 2004, Revised Edition 2007"

Cover Illustration by Matthew M. Finn

www.finngalleries.com

LILY SERENA DIPREE

TALES OF THE TRAVELING TEMPTRESS
AN EROTIC NOVEL

2008

Tales of the Traveling Temptress

CONTENTS

To the adventurer: tickle your sexual fancy and open yourself to new experiences.

As individuals we all must choose which road to take in life. We have a choice to be either who we truly are, or to be what others want us to be. As for me, I courageously accept who I am and who I will become. I am on a quest to sate my unquenchable thirst for sexual pleasure. Follow me, as I explore the temptations of passion to its fullest. From a chance meeting with a stranger, an erotic strip tease, the infamous wedding party, a rough-hewn motorcyclist, a naughty swinging couple: these are just a few of the exploits you will take pleasure in. Delve into these pages and delight in my journey.

Love,

The Temptress

This Book Is Dedicated To Those Who Allow The Art Of Sexual Experience To Awaken Their Hidden Desires. To J.R. Whose Unflagging Support Will Always Be Remembered. And To Kristal Who Kept My Pen To Paper, Even At 3:00 In The Morning When Normal People Are Sleeping.

PROLOGUE

Beach Bunny

It was a sweltering day and as the sun beat down, I felt my backside burning. I had been lying on the beach for hours and beads of sweat trickled endlessly between my breasts. My thoughts had been adrift all afternoon: I'd pondered one thing, then another, and yet, just as sleep threatened to overtake my overheated body, I was roused by the steps of someone approaching.

As the footfalls got closer my excitement grew. I was certain that no one had seen me leave home this morning, and since I lived in an upscale part of town, I felt secure in my surroundings. I'd know soon enough who drew near so I stayed put, alert but not alarmed.

Abruptly, a man knelt down beside me. I didn't recognize the smell of his cologne, and no words passed between us. Unexpectedly, his hand grazed the back of my thigh, causing shivers to run throughout my body. His fingertips moved gently up and down the backs of my legs, tickling me. Caution told me to turn over and slap whoever had touched me uninvited, but I couldn't. I lay frozen in the moment, my senses energized.

The stranger's transgressions continued, causing my heart to quicken its pace. With one hand he stroked and fondled my thighs, while with his other he worked quickly to untie my swim top, forcing my full breasts to their natural shape as my suit melded with the towel. Heavy sighs escaped his lips and tantalized my skin. I squirmed, feeling goose-bumps form on my flesh as I anticipated his next move. Grabbing my right hand, he folded his fingers between mine. My desire rose, a heavy pull of passion stirring from deep within.

The man must have sensed my excitement, for now he let go of my hand and took hold of my swimsuit bottom. In a single motion he tore it from my body, leaving me naked on my towel. Ensconced in my role as a pawn, I played the game, allowing him to do as he pleased with my body. I had read books about situations like this, but at this very moment, I was experiencing the reality: pleasure and pain, passion and trepidation. Unyielding delight tortured me.

My thoughts were jumbled when my towel shifted from the weight of the stranger's body as he lay down next to me. The heat of his breath against my skin sent relentless tingly waves through my loins. Following the line of my spine he began to kiss every inch of my back, from the crest of my neck down to the crevice of my ass, where he stopped briefly to turn me over.

I kept my eyes shut to heighten my arousal. I didn't want to know who tempted my senses. I didn't want my vision distorted by reality. I wanted only to fall victim to his touch, to his hands that roamed my body tirelessly.

When he fondled my breasts, my nipples grew stiff, jutting outward, craving his attention. I trembled and my intimate juices flowed. I licked my lips as he placed one hand between my legs, but when he slipped a finger in between my nether lips, I bit my bottom lip hard.

Having started this adventure feeling horny and excited, my feelings now bordered on reckless abandon. And knowing that he was looking at my fully unclad form only heightened my eagerness.

Emboldened by my passion, I grabbed his hands from between my legs. I wanted to feel him inside me. Swiftly I moved atop him and fumbled with his belt until I was able to pull out his semierect member and stroke him up and down, experiencing his growing girth within my clutch. One hand tight around his dick, I began kissing him on the chest, first taking his nipples into my mouth, and then pinching them between my fingers.

Purposefully, I moved down his body. I licked the tip of his engorged length, traced random patterns with my nimble tongue around the head of his shaft, and then dipped into the tiny fissure at the tip. His arousal leaked from him with every pulse of his prick, inflaming my desire. It was apparent that he wanted me, but I whispered, "Only when I'm ready."

I managed to keep the tip of his cock in my mouth while I used one hand to stroke him and the other to caress his balls. I felt him grow swollen and tight, and knew he was almost ready to erupt. I didn't want the saltiness of his cum in my mouth; I wanted instead to feel him enfolded within me. I wanted my pussy to sear his dick, so that he could find release only after he had driven his shaft fully within me, quenching my lust.

Instinctively I straddled him, teasing him with my clit. I rubbed myself against him until sweet anguish overtook me and I sat down on his thick, throbbing cock. First my movements were slow and tentative, but quickly my pace turned fast and furious. I forced him to drive rigorously, fully, deeply into my grasping depths. My muscles tightened around his turgid cock, and I gyrated on his body, rising and falling, fucking him as if I had known him for years. "Oh yeah, fuck me, don't stop, oh fuck, I'm coming!" I screamed, as languorous warmth suffused my body and the waves of my climax swept over me. In unison with me, he too exploded, unleashing with such force that he had to pull my ass tightly down to him and hold himself deep inside my quivering walls.

The sound of a low-flying airplane forced my eyes open. No man lay next to me. I was alone. Wiping the sweat from my brow with one hand, I pulled the other from inside my swimsuit bottoms and sighed, "God, what a great prologue for my memoirs."

With a giggle, I rose and walked to the water's edge. Slowly, I eased my body into the surf and dove into the depths of the sea. When I had finally cooled my senses, I left the waves and returned to my beckoning laptop. To my amazement, my imagined one-on-one liaison had inspired me. Finally, I knew how to describe my past in a way that would entice others to follow me through my sensual journey of sexual exploration.

And this is how it all began...

CHAPTER 1

My sexual escapades truly began the summer I graduated from high school. My brother and I reveled in luxury while our jet-setting parents celebrated their freedom, half a world away. In the absence of parental guidance, I learned to embrace the full scope of my female wiles. I knew I could seduce anyone I chose. One Friday evening, I targeted my brother's best friend.

All-American Pastime

Friday evenings were usually girls' night out, but tonight my sights were set on entertaining my brother's best friend, Bryan, who was waiting for my brother to arrive home. Countless times my brother had warned me to steer clear of his lecherous friends, but when his phone call alerted me to his car troubles, I disregarded his warnings.

Knowing that I had plenty of time before my brother returned, I decided to make my move. I knew right from wrong, but Bryan's burly biceps mesmerized me. My stomach quivered as I imagined his athletic body against the background of my bed sheets. Brazenly I strode across the room and playfully spanked Bryan on the ass. His muscles tensed instantly, and as he turned around, he flashed me his All-American smile.

Unexpectedly, he grabbed my waist and pulled me tight against him, murmuring against my (at the time) sandy blonde curls, "Do you want to take this past teasing?"

"Oh yeah," I gasped hungrily, as his hands grazed down my back, leaving a trail of fire in their wake.

In one swift movement Bryan flung me over his shoulder and stalked down the hall toward my bedroom. He tore back the comforter on my bed, laid me on the smooth black satin sheets, and whispered softly, "Stay still."

I didn't like taking orders, but I wanted Bryan, no matter what. And if that meant taking an order or two, I was up for it.

"You've been teasing me for weeks about your blindfold. Does it really exist? I mean, is it fact or fiction?" Bryan asked huskily.

"Fact," I purred.

"I'll lock the front door, you put it on."

My body flooded with excitement. As soon as he had left the room I stood, stripped off my clothing, walked to my dresser, and pulled out my drawer full of erotic toys. On top a black blindfold lay amid cords of silk, lotions, and movies. "You only live once," I chuckled, grabbing the blindfold and a cord.

I lay down on the bed, tied the blindfold into place, and scooted back into the pillows, arranging the cord beside me. Anticipation surged through me as I visualized Bryan fucking me. I heard him draw near. In the darkness my senses homed in on his ragged breathing, which increased my desire. I listened while he shed his clothing.

My nipples tightened as my hands traced their firm buds. I slid my hands down my stomach in tiny increments until they nestled in my patch of crisp curls. My fingers caressed my horny hollow. Squirming with delight, I stroked my clit, succumbing to this next escapade in my sexual odyssey.

Hoping to fuel Bryan's desire, I continued to flick my clit rapidly with my right index finger while I inserted the first two fingers of my left hand deep into my moistened sheath. With every masturbating stroke, Bryan's moans echoed through the room.

"Tired of being the audience?" I asked, pulling my hands teasingly away.

"Matter of fact," he replied, climbing onto the bed and straddling me, "I enjoyed your presentation so much, I want an encore. Some audience participation would be nice this time."

With that, Bryan drew my hands above my head and tied them loosely with the silken cord.

I was blind and immobile, totally at Bryan's mercy. My breath caught. I shuddered as I awaited the onslaught of his sexual touch. "Please pleasure me now," I begged.

Bryan obeyed. He began fondling me, rubbing his hands and fingers all over my body, his mouth greedily feasting upon my nipples.

I felt as though my body were laid out as his banquet. His lips left my nipples, which had served as appetizers, and he headed for the main course: the delectable wetness between my thighs. His agile tongue devoured my softness—licking, teasing and nibbling my velvety smooth hood.

Suddenly he stopped, leaving me breathless. I felt his hands grasp the back of my head. His lips brushed lightly against my ear lobe. "Don't speak unless you're spoken to. I'm going to tease your senses with three different items. Each thing you identify will force me to do as you wish. However, if you guess wrong, you must do whatever I say. Still game?"

"Oh God yes," I cried.

Flinching in apprehension, I listened to the rustling of a paper bag, and then felt tiny droplets of cool liquid on my feet. I squirmed as Bryan's fingers glided between each delicate digit, then kneaded the tense arch of my foot. With both hands he stimulated every inch of my flesh from the tips of my toes to the top of one silken thigh where he stopped purposefully, inches from my glistening lips, then moved smoothly back down the other leg.

I was exhilarated. Yet, just when I thought he had finished his massage, more droplets trailed the length of my upraised arms. Bryan's hands rubbed slickly through my fingers, then down to the hollow of my neck where the essence of lavender filled the air. Smiling, I realized that Bryan had grabbed my body oil off the counter in the kitchen.

"You think you know, Ms. Smiling Face?" Bryan asked.

"Oil."

"Be specific."

"My lavender body oil that was in the kitchen."

"I'm your slave. What do you desire?"

"Torture my clit with your tongue."

I felt the heat of his breath against my flesh, and when his tongue flickered against my inner thigh my legs fell open, demanding his devoted touch. Bryan's tongue lapped my sweet nectar while his hands rubbed my smooth ass. His tongue continued in a small but steady circular motion. My ass clenched, welcoming my climax. I moaned, "Yes…oh yes…you nasty boy."

Abruptly, Bryan stopped. "I told you not to speak unless spoken to. Since you broke the rules, it's my turn."

I felt abandoned. My body ached for fulfillment. The exquisite oral pleasure Bryan had delivered had left me only licks away from an earth-shattering orgasm. I was in torment, left in a state bordering on frantic.

"Okay, next item," Bryan said, prying me from my licentious thoughts. "Open your mouth."

Following orders promptly, I parted my lips, and relished the firm sweetness of what could only be a perfect strawberry.

"What is that?" Bryan inquired.

"An amazing strawberry."

"Right again. What's your pleasure?"

"Release me from my bondage so I can sit on your face while I give you the blowjob of your life."

My hands fell free, and I felt Bryan lie beside me on the bed. Without untying my blindfold, I carefully mounted his face, finding his tongue eagerly awaiting my sex. Letting out a garbled sigh, I leaned forward, searching Bryan's skin with anxious kisses until I felt his hardness pulse beneath my lips. Enveloping him in my mouth, I felt the head of his cock grow tight, and with each suck he released the pre-cum of his desire.

As his tongue teased the inside walls of my pussy, I pulled his cock slowly into and out of my mouth. Every maddening flick of his tongue made my clit throb for more, until my muffled moans flooded the room. "Oh...oh...yes...that's it... oh fuck...yeah!" I came in relentless waves as his swollen tip exploded inside my mouth.

When my breathing had slowed, I assumed my former prone position. Exhausted, but far from finished, I licked my lips, tasting the carnage I had created.

The bed jostled. "OK. One last item." Bryan cajoled.

"But how will you give me what I want if I guess this time?" I asked coyly.

"What do you mean?"

"You just shot your load, so how will you be able to fuck me when I guess correctly?"

"Just looking at your naked body makes my dick hard. And thinking of fucking you? Well, just guess."

I imagined Bryan would choose something challenging to tempt me with; the intrigue stirred me.

"What is it?" Bryan asked as a liquid ran across my stomach, a strong aroma rising from its passage.

"Liquor, I think."

"Oh, come on. You can do better than that."

"Try it on another part of my body."

Bryan's fingers traced the outline of my lips and I grinned. "You sly devil...you snagged the bottle of Baileys from the liquor cabinet. I know I'm right, so give me what I want. Fuck me. Fuck me hard!"

I tore off the blindfold and pulled Bryan onto me. Clutching his ass, I squirmed as his cock nudged against the gossamer silk of my pussy, demanding entrance. When he delved into my wetness, deeper and deeper, harder and harder, I shuddered.

My body burned with incandescent fire as Bryan rode me to monumental heights. His vein-laden cock moved with skillful determination. His hands angled my hips for deeper penetration. He gripped my ass tightly, attempting to penetrate me with greater force, and I held him inside as he rolled over, swapping our positions.

Now on top, I had control. I raised and lowered myself on his cock, writhing atop him as my head thrashed from side to side. I screamed, swore, and fucked him as if I owed him money, while my tits bounced in rhythm with each of my violent gyrations. I sailed through my climax; all the while Bryan continued to plunge into my intoxicating abyss until my muscles had sucked the essence from him.

Mutually satisfied, we collapsed: soaked in shared sweat, spent versions of our former selves, every ounce of energy lost to us. But before I had the chance to ask who had really won the game, a pounding on the front door echoed through the house.

CHAPTER 2

Everyone knows that the Deep South holds sultry promises within its magnolia-scented air. This perfume is one that lingers, hidden in the depths of a man's mind until a wicked, teasing glance from a Southern belle releases an elusive memory of utmost hidden pleasures.

While visiting my best friend down South, I decided as a lark to seduce the owner of the neighboring plantation. Unbeknownst to me, my friend, who worked for Lance as his executive assistant, had watched me that day and took note of the entire seduction. The following erotic tale is based on how she envisioned Lance might have recollected his time with me on that sensual summer day.

Steel Magnolias

It was a sweltering day, the heavy air permeated with the essence of magnolias as Lance sat in his study reviewing the daily assignments that went hand in hand with running the company. The air conditioning was on the blink, and, leaning back in his wingback desk chair, Lance noticed that his trousers clung to his thighs, while the sweat on his brow trickled down his cheek. His shirt had long since been unbuttoned and discarded. Working alone did have its advantages.

Lance spent his bachelor nights toying with women and his professional days carefully planning his next financial coup. His continued success in business depended on his never letting his guard down. Today's heat apparently had blurred his focus and as a tropical breeze billowed through the drapes the sweet scent of magnolias wafted around his study.

Drawn from his thoughts by the sudden change in atmosphere, Lance turned in his chair and pulled back the gauze curtains to gaze into the garden. What lay before his eyes: a divine vision. A memo on his desk had informed him of the new gardener, but outside his window stood nothing less than a goddess—a creature between humankind and the angels.

Lance sat spellbound as this enchanting woman stepped up the rungs of a ladder on the terrace, apparently to tend the flowers that hung from the arbor. The tight-fitting bodice of her white sundress enhanced the silhouette of her full and supple breasts. The gods had graced him; as the sun beat down, he saw more and more of her incredible form revealed through her sheer, flowing skirts. She was all woman. This flamboyant, yet delectable, woman didn't fit the description of what one would call a Southern lady born and bred. Southern ladies rarely came across as so unabashedly sexual.

Lance sat idly watching, feeling the rise of heaviness in his loins. Just as the woman lifted her arm, stretching up to water the hanging plants, a gust of wind hoisted her skirts, exposing a trimmed nest of curls between her thighs. Lance stood involuntarily. Now his arousal compelled him to act; he could no longer remain confined in his chair. A shudder racked his body. His release beckoned.

Lance pushed his chair under the desk. His work would wait; his need would not. He had been watching her almost like a voyeur. Hell, he *was* a voyeur. He observed how her lips moved, as if she were singing. He hastened to the terrace doors, to hear the sound of her voice.

The doors swung open and instantly the sweet-voiced siren initiated the most erotic experience of his life. A voice like hers haunted the daydreams of every Southern man: husky and low, with a soft Georgian drawl. The embodiment of most men's fantasies stood before him and would soon be his to worship. Closing his eyes, taking in the sounds of passion she released, his body rocked slowly, mesmerized in sweet torment.

Bewitched, he opened his eyes and stalked towards her like a predator: slowly, calculating, unnoticed. His hands reached out eagerly towards the explicit promise of her body and gently grazed her flesh. A sigh, released in conjunction with his touch, flowed from her mouth, forcing his already engorged member to throb with visible pulses.

She didn't turn to face him. Instead, she climbed higher up the ladder, exposing more of her flesh to him. She didn't seem afraid or inhibited, but she wasn't offering herself either. She was cunning as a vixen, and Lance's excitement grew by the second. She had given him an unspoken go-ahead. He understood that while she wanted to be taken, it was important in the South for a woman to retain her image of chastity.

Lance's six foot three frame meant that he didn't need to climb the ladder in order to reach her. He just leaned forward, slid his hands up her dress and grabbed her hips. He kissed the roundness of her tanned, bare buttocks, pausing briefly to inhale her womanly scent. Her growing arousal became obvious as he lightly caressed her moistening flesh. Lance raised his head and was about to bury his face in the crease of her bare thighs, when she turned slowly, sliding her bottom down onto the ladder step. Her move forced his face into the mound that held the blossom of her youth and beauty.

He took her golden thighs in his arms and positioned them on either side of his shoulders. Then he moved his mouth into position and began gently licking the tight nub at the top of her sex. Her delicate flesh grew wetter with each strike of his soft tongue. His movements became more intense, and then stopped, teasingly. Lance knew how to please a woman, so when he again suckled on her clit, she began moaning and her thighs began to quiver. Suddenly, with feline grace, he looked up and winked, then turned and sauntered back to his study.

She lowered herself down the ladder and followed him. Now she had entered his kingdom, so he turned from seducer to marauder, pushing her up against the wall to gain leverage. Effortlessly, he lifted her. Once she had wrapped her legs around his neck, he ripped the buttons from the front of her dress, leaving her bare and fully exposed. Her muscles tightened under his tongue and her harried breathing indicated her mounting passion. Her body arched back and, digging her nails into his shoulders, she rasped, "Now! Please now!"

Wanting to experience her body completely, Lance inserted two of his long fingers into the tight sheath of her warm, moist fissure, torturing her with a quick flick of his tongue, then pulled away and lowered her to the floor. He stood above her as she lay naked, and he could see that she was just waiting to be devoured. Without hesitation, he unleashed his thick, throbbing, member from his pants and joined her on the floor, pushing apart her thighs with his knees.

His shaft pulsed, preparing to penetrate her dampened furrow, but first she reached out and fully unfastened his trousers, pushing them down with her toes. Now unclothed, Lance could no longer stand the torture of being separate. Her beauty overwhelmed him. Her full lips beckoned him to kiss them, her sapphire blue eyes mesmerized him, and her hair cascading over her shoulders in a waterfall of chestnut curls trapped him. He was completely bewitched, totally under her spell.

Lance positioned himself above her and, in one fluid motion, drove his cock fully within her. Her velvet sheath closed snugly around him, and the heated friction forced moans to escape their lips in unison. With each of his undulating thrusts, her flesh ensconced his.

The sensation he delivered, pulling out of her and then plunging back in with a twist of his hips brought her to climax within moments. For the first time, he heard her scream, "Oh fuck! Yes!" Lance rode through her waves of release and, as her muscles tortured him in a clenching grip, his motions became faster and harder.

Knowing she had reached fulfillment, Lance gave her no time to catch her breath, but pulled her over on top of him and commanded, "Ride me. Ride me hard."

A wicked smile crossed her lips. She positioned her feet under his ass, sat straight up with her hands behind her, and began to play with his balls. Her nipples stood erect, begging for attention. Not wanting to lose his position in the moment by leaning up to take them in his mouth, Lance pinched each nipple hard, once and again. Then he licked his fingers and pinched her nipples more, teasing her senses by rolling the tight buds between his fingers. He reached out with his left hand and pulled her right hand to join him. "A woman who's capable of giving herself pleasure, surely can pleasure me," he said playfully.

Appearing to be up for his game, she used her right hand to massage one breast while her left hand toyed with his balls. All the while, her body's momentum didn't halt. Once his voyeuristic needs were satisfied, Lance pulled her hands away and laid them to rest on his chest. With her newly found leverage, she lifted herself up off his rock-hard cock—just far enough to tease him wickedly. Then, as quickly as she had risen, she dropped back down onto him, forcing him to groan with lust. Every moan that passed his lips made her quicken her ride.

Lance grabbed her ass with both his hands and began moving her back and forth on top of him. As she clenched her inner muscles, keeping him deep within her, her ass tensed, provoking him to lift his hand and spank her. At first he struck her softly, but as her craving became apparent, he slapped her more forcefully. Her moans urged Lance's hunger on. Pulling her closer, he cupped her ass in his hands, lifting her up and then down hard on him. He had full control of the speed of their bodies slapping in the friction-formed heat.

Lance's instincts took over. His hips lunged upward of their own accord while he clutched her to him, bucking her body upon his wildly thrusting pelvis. They were one being, as primal instincts ignited into an inferno of need. Her tits bounced in front of his face, slapping him. Her body quivered and contracted with the force of her release, pushing him over the brink. As a cry of intense satisfaction flooded the room, his climax exploded inside her. Together they collapsed in the sex-scented air.

As their breathing began to slow, Lance turned her to lie beside him. He knew he was in trouble because *she* was trouble. Her beauty had snared him. As he tenderly lifted her head and placed it on his chest, she said, "By the way, I'm visiting next door, and it's been a pleasure making your acquaintance."

Lance laughed. Then gathering her hair in one hand and lifting her chin to peer into her eyes with the other, he replied, "The pleasure's been all mine. I'm honored you stopped by."

CHAPTER 3

During my college years my parents passed away in an automobile accident. Their untimely death left my brother and me sole heirs to their substantial estate. Attaining financial freedom allowed me to pursue a lighthearted existence. I found myself participating in many different avenues of enjoyment; one of my favorites became the seduction of powerful men.

Now I fondly recall the memory of my girlfriend's wedding, and the pleasure of experiencing her uncle in a rewarding sexual interlude guaranteed to boost my ego. Here's to Uncle Brock—a cowboy to be remembered.

Bucking Bronco

Exhausted, I lounged back in the tub. My eyes grew heavy as the water rose up over my legs, caressing my body and teasing my senses. I grinned as memories of my rapturous rendezvous with Brock Swanson flooded my mind. Knowing that his flawless body lay sleeping on the other side of the door, I relished the thought that his dreams were filled with me. We had just shared sheer perfection, and my wildest schoolgirl fantasies seemed to pale in comparison. "What a perfect ending to a glorious day," I thought aloud.

A buzz of gossip filled the room when the infamous "Uncle Brock" had strolled into the chapel early that morning. What a specimen: perfect, as if he had stepped right out of a motion-picture screen. He introduced himself to everyone, smiling each time he took someone's hand.

During our introduction my sex had grown moist and tingly the instant he clasped my hand. His fingers were long; his rugged hands well weathered and calloused. At that moment I had remembered Sheila telling me about her uncle who rode bucking broncos for a living down in Texas. The roughness of his hands turned me on, and I imagined what it would be like to have him holding my hair tight behind my head.

I knew instantly that we wouldn't have just a one-night stand. Although the touch of his hands first drew me to him, I fell for the whole package: the way he held himself, his aura, and his physique.

Brock stood at least six foot six, and even in my three-inch heels, at a lofty five foot nine, I measured just above nipple level on his chest. He wore a black tux that showed off his eminent stature. His white dress shirt fit snugly under the jacket, and instead of the traditional tie and cummerbund, a turquoise arrowhead bolo tie rested against the crisp lines. His trousers hung against well-worn, black cowboy boots. His gray eyes transported me to another realm, one where he reigned as grand magician and I served as his sorceress.

Throughout the entire wedding ceremony my eyes did not stray from his. Our connection held me in thrall like a trance. I tried to concentrate on the nuptials, but I could only visualize making hot, passionate love to Brock. I vowed that if I got the chance I would break this cowboy's record. I would hold onto him, wrap my arms around his back, swathe his body within mine and tame him with my sweet favors.

The sun disappeared as the service ended. As we all left the hall for the parlor, I sensed that Brock's smoldering sensuality tempted every woman present, but he remained by my side, his amorous attention just for me. I took a long, deep breath, growing familiar with his subtle personal scent and his cologne. There were things about him that I couldn't wait to find out, places on his body I longed to explore and devour.

I felt like Cinderella at the ball, swaying back and forth to the music with Brock holding me. My emerald satin sheath dress clung seductively to my every curve and my (currently) fiery bloom of cascading red locks flowed down my back, enhancing my pert breasts and shapely ass.

When Brock rested his hand on mine and squeezed, I sensed he had read my mind. His touch seared through my veins, assuring me that before the end of the evening I would know his body and soul intimately. Erotic images invaded my mind, and my eyelids closed tightly. Tempted by thoughts of fantasy sex I felt warmth trickle between my thighs. My inner muscles clenched at the emptiness within, hungering to have him inside me.

My restless hands searched until they found refuge on Brock's chiseled buttocks. Greedily absorbing the feel of his suddenly tightened muscles, they slipped down the backside of his legs. A low, husky moan echoed in my ear. I eyed the crowd and the people mingling, entangled in their private worlds. I knew I had to take a chance, to experience the vortex of feeling that I would find in his arms. Our eyes met and set fire in a language all our own. I slipped away from Brock and out the door, allowing my fingers to graze his palm.

Everyone in the wedding party had their own cabins, so when I turned left up the walkway, Brock pulled me by the hand toward the right. My legs grew weak and my mind anxious as we approached his cabin. My desire rose, immobilizing my mind. My lips parted eagerly, giving way to his tongue when he took my face in his hands and raised my mouth to his. Low, whimpering moans ebbed from my lips as the heat of his kiss coursed through me.

Brock drew me up into his arms, kicked open the door and carried me over the threshold. Inside, he lowered me to the bed. His lips clung to mine, and I gave in to my breathless sweet torment. My fingers worked swiftly to loosen his bolo tie and undo his buttons until his shirt slipped off over his broad shoulders.

My hands skated over the bronzed perfection of his bare chest. I took his right nipple between my lips and sucked wantonly on his flesh, while I fondled his left nipple between my fingers. My lips ventured leisurely downward, and he flexed beneath my touch, moaning without restraint. With my determined tongue, I traced a path to the arrow of hair at the top of Brock's pants, my hands masterfully tugging them away from his skin. My teeth tore at his trousers until the top button popped and I could ease the zipper down.

"Oh baby," I sighed, finding him naked beneath. Purposefully, I shimmied his slacks down, pausing momentarily to tickle the tip of his silken rod with my tongue. The sheer size of his monstrous member rising erect before me whetted my appetite. I turned, posing my backside toward it.

I ached. Only his touch could fuel the flames burning within my loins. I needed him to dance within my depths, assuaging my need. Brock sat up and began lightly kissing my neck. I shivered, overwrought, while he skillfully released each button on my dress. His energy passed through to me, the volatile friction of his fingers electrified my newly bared flesh.

The feel of his hands caressing my shoulders, and then gliding down the middle of my back, tortured me. Goose-bumps formed as I watched him push the tiny straps over my shoulders. When I rose from the bed, my dress instantly pooled about my ankles. Slowly, I stepped out of the coil of silken fabric and faced Brock.

I felt gloriously sexy in my lingerie, and the extra effort I had taken that morning putting on matching panties, garter belt and corset now paid off. He signaled his approval by licking first his top lip, then the bottom. His lustful gaze roved across my form. My eyes must have conveyed that I wanted him to make the first move, for he impulsively secured me to his body, close enough that I could feel the beating of his heart.

Earlier that evening, I had wanted to tame this bronco. Now, as he stood before me like a force of nature, beckoning me to him, I wanted to stay in the saddle forever. I felt his pulse rage as he breathed raggedly into my ear. I nibbled his neck, and a moan full of ache and desire rumbled from his throat. He boldly pushed me back onto the bed. Carefully he unhinged my garters. My body shuddered beneath his touch. He tenderly rolled my stockings down the length of my legs, stopping to nibble on the backs of my ankles, and then eagerly nudged apart my knees.

Every touch Brock delivered to my sensitive skin energized my movements. He glided his way back up my body, and then placing a hand on each side of my white silk panties, shimmied them down over my curves. "Oh, Brock," escaped from my lips as he kissed me hard on the mouth; no tongue this time, only lips.

My corset was the final article separating us, and I didn't want anything to come between us. I reached behind my back and released the clasps, freeing my breasts, my nipples pert and budding.

Brock's scalding gaze produced a craving in me that made me want to cry out. Never had I relished in such blissful sensations from foreplay; it was as if I were at the zenith of a roller-coaster ride. I clutched his stiff evidence of desire in my right hand while my left eased between my thighs, parting my lips and wetting his entrance. All the while, Brock watched intently as I fondled and toyed with my pussy.

He didn't need help finding my warm and inviting opening. Instead, his dick executed a personal attack, penetrating me slowly. I responded by raising my hips, grabbing his ass and pulling him forcefully into me. He buried his thick shaft deep within my core and together we moved in ancient rhythm.

I met his every plunge with an undulation of my own. Each time he teased me by withdrawing his dick then driving deeper into me, I dug my nails into his ass and spanked him playfully. My breasts bounced, and my ass squeezed tight as I clenched my intimate cleft like a liquid vice around the trunk of his sex.

With sweat beading on his forehead, Brock's facial expressions grew more intense with my every contraction. I spanked him briskly now, panting, "Fuck me, cowboy. Ride me like the wind." Passion ascending, Brock's lust poured forth. Shimmering in a mist of sweat, he slammed his pelvis against mine. When I could stand no more, I cried out, "Oh. Don't stop. Please don't stop. Oh God, I'm coming!"

Brock's pace quickened. His body heaving, he took hold of my hips, clasped me to him, and groaned gutturally, "Oh fuck yeah, you feisty filly," through clenched teeth as he emptied his seed deep within me.

Exhausted and boneless, I melded with the sheets as Brock collapsed on top of me. On our first sexual encounter, we had climaxed together. Gently, Brock lowered his lips to mine and kissed me tenderly before moving to lie next to me. He brushed my hair away from my sweat-covered brow. Before he closed his eyes, he whispered softly, "You're the first filly I've ever wanted to break in. Hope we can practice all night?"

A stirring from the other side of the bathroom door alerted me to the sexy naked man waiting in bed for me. I smiled as I pulled the plug on the tub, stood up and peered into the mirror. My hair had a tousled, just-fucked look, but I felt I looked better than ever. Pulling a towel around my waist, I giggled, "Time for round four, sleepyhead, here I come."

CHAPTER 4

Ever wonder what it is about birthdays? "Over the hill" syndrome sets in, and the whole world drops out from beneath you. The insecurities surrounding those turning point birthdays bring up all sorts of depression.

This tale is dedicated to Tristan, a one-time love whom I helped nurse back up his imaginary hill. Although he had just turned forty, I showed him that not all was lost. The randy teenager within was still alive and ready to play.

Birthday Wonder

I couldn't understand why Tristan spent the morning of his fortieth birthday sulking. However, while he wallowed in midlife crisis, tangled up in the "age" thing, I'd gone out shopping.

When I returned, I found Tristan at the kitchen table, moping, staring at his beer. "Caught ya," I said, as I dropped my shopping bags on the counter.

When he didn't respond, I handed him another beer. "Still worrying about the over-the-hill stuff?" Although he didn't smile, I straddled his lap. "Oh come on. You still have your hair, your big dick, and me."

He cocked his head. "Okay. You're right about the hair. And you're always a sex magnet, but—

"No buts. Get up and get dressed. I'm taking you out for your birthday and *you* don't have a choice."

I dressed to entice him. My sensual shoulder-length blonde tresses were pulled up tight in a ponytail, giving me the image of a perky cheerleader. My skintight, low-cut, black dress clung to my every curve. My buttocks blossomed into an inverted heart, and my waist tapered in, then rose to meet the pert plumpness of my breasts. I wore no stockings with my heels—only the golden hue of the sun caressed my skin. My nerve endings began to tingle as Tristan surveyed the length of my body, his heated amber gaze scorching me.

Slowly I headed for the stairs, but Tristan grabbed me and turned me to face him. His hands skated across the bared flesh of my shoulders. Then, tightening his arms, he sheltered me in his ardent embrace. I smiled, feeling his hardness grow against my flimsy clothes.

"I promise your birthday wishes will be fulfilled, but for now, this will have to do." I leaned in, pressing my budding nipples against the masculine hardness of his chest, and kissed him with promise. My tongue traced the outline of his lips before delving between them. Feverishly, his tongue frolicked with mine in erotic play. My hands drifted the length of his chiseled torso, stopping only when the ridge of his manhood, straining against the denim of his jeans, involuntarily pulsed at my touch. Teasing, I pulled away. "Let's go."

"Where are we going?" he inquired with exaggerated innocence.

"RJ's," I answered.

"The strip club?"

"Yep. You've been pleading with me for months, so I decided for your birthday we'd go. You need to be stripped of your negative attitude and this is just the thing. Now go," I demanded, pointing to the car.

When we arrived I headed straight for the doorman with Tristan following in my wake. "I made reservations with Chuck. I paid for everything in advance," I said.

"Go on in," he instructed. "Scott will help you. He's the bartender, the one with the ponytail."

Pat Benatar's "Hit Me with Your Best Shot" screamed through the speakers with a deafening echo. "Two shots of tequila with Corona chasers," I shouted. The bartender nodded.

After the bartender had set down our drinks, I turned to Tristan, "Chuck reserved a table for us in the front."

When we located our reserved seats, Tristan set the drinks on the table and pulled my chair out for me. "What's really going on here?" he asked taking a seat next to me.

Amused by his bewilderment, I ran my long, nimble fingers up his inner thigh, reviving his manhood under my touch. "I wanted tonight to be extra special," I said, turning around to eye the room. "I don't know about you, but I'm getting wet just imagining who's going to get naked first."

His arousal thumped in sudden excitement, straining against his zipper. With a lick of my lips and a saucy grin, I aided him in unleashing his growing fury by parting his tight denim and charming his silken snake from its enclosure.

Tristan's thick shaft jumped as I curled my fingers around it. I toyed with him mischievously, and his masculine essence gathered at his crown. He pushed back against the chair to enhance his pleasure, moistening my hand to aid my motions.

"Are you ready for our first dancer?" a man with a microphone yelled, pushing past them.

Jostled, Tristan quickly rubbed the fluid from the tip of his dick and rapidly restored it within the protective bonds of his pants.

Putting our hands together along with the crowd, we thundered our anticipatory applause. The first dancer strolled out wearing a bright lemon yellow bikini top and a tight black miniskirt. I licked my lips. Turning, I watched as Tristan's face flushed with excitement.

The dancer had unzipped her skirt, and as her hips swayed back and forth, it fell to the floor. Turning sideways to the crowd, she stepped out of the skirt, then bent over and ran her hands daringly up the back of her thighs. Once her hands met the roundness of her ass, she reached behind her back and unhinged her top, which fell instantly to the floor. Only a tiny matching yellow G-string covered her as she walked to the end of the runway, where she jiggled her tits in Tristan's face, then walked off the stage.

"Very nice seats," Tristan said, flashing a lusty grin.

"Thought you'd like 'em."

The next two dancers were a blur. Tristan had slipped his hand up my dress and along my thigh, my nakedness inviting his touch. He gently rubbed the outer lips of my sex and my secret softness blossomed like the petals of an opening flower. He eased into me with his long middle finger while his thumb massaged the core of my burgeoning desire.

I writhed beneath his agile finger-play. The tender friction was making my sultry sweet moisture begin to flow. With the crowd engrossed in the show, no one noticed what pleasures Tristan was bestowing on me under our table skirt. The room around me ceased to exist. The sexual frustration I had felt at the beginning of this evening would be quenched. My eyes drifted shut, and my body moved to the rhythm of the music that surrounded me. My hips instinctively met every delving thrust of Tristan's fingers. My inner muscles tightly clasped against him, adding to my pleasure. The unbearable tension that gripped me exploded just as the crowd's wild applause roared their appreciation of the departing dancer.

I knew that Tristan's sexual release was imminent when he growled, "Down your drink, we're leaving," his voice husky with need.

"Oh come on," I whimpered teasingly.

"Now!" Tristan demanded as his drink quickly disappeared and he stood up.

Instead of fighting him, I lifted my glass to my lips and gulped down my beer. Tristan closed in behind me, lifted me up over one shoulder, and without a word walked toward the front door. As he pushed it open and carried me out into the night, I shivered with a desperate hunger. By the time we reached the car, desire was indisputable and my passion undeniable.

Tristan took my face in his hands and searched my eyes. I wanted him. Now. Here in the car, in the parking lot. I couldn't wait until we were one. I was naked within moments of entering the vehicle. Completely unveiled, I scooted back against the door. I put my right leg up on the dashboard and my left over the seat, exposing my scalding softness in its entirety, begging him without words to ease the hollow ache within me.

Elementally male, Tristan hastily discarded his shirt and unzipped his pants, freeing his turgid shaft. Releasing a guttural growl, he leaned forward and buried his face between my thighs.

The first flick of his tongue parted my feminine folds. He inserted one finger into my smooth channel, while his thumb found and teased the nub of my rapture and my body succumbed to sweet oblivion. Each time his finger glided into my body, my ass tightened, urging his movements to hurry.

Shifting, I maneuvered myself into position on top of him. Tristan's cock throbbed, pressing against my moist sheath, begging admission. He entered me with a swift swing of his hips, and my playful pussy closed around him, securing us together. I squeezed my muscles to hold him deep, caressing his length with moist heat. He lifted me up, sliding completely out of me, and then pulled my hips tightly back down upon him. His dick swelled, filling my body, and as I rocked my hips, my velvet nub rubbed against the rough abrasion of his tight curls.

I dug my nails into Tristan's brawny thighs and watched as his thick cock glided in and out of me. My hard-tipped breasts swung in motion, and my strangled gasps of, "Oh yeah. Don't stop. You feel so good," echoed through the car.

Tristan pumped harder. My wet pussy lubricated his every stroke, until he could no longer hold back and he exploded in bliss. Intense pulses of completion flowed endlessly from him as his head pushed against the seat and his hands greedily kept me atop him. He shifted my ass back and forth, not allowing me to move away until his entire seed had been spent.

I laid my head on his sweat-drenched shoulder knowing that the wait had been well worth it, and we hadn't even opened the gifts yet.

CHAPTER 5

I have spent many evenings tasting the pleasures that powerful men have to offer me. But I am aware that men are like wine, and if you overindulge, you will surely pay the penalty in the morning. Seeing how I'm used to capturing my prey, then discarding it before an attachment forms I became disheartened when I fell for "Charles," one of my conquests who happened to have a wife.

I am a strong willed and determined woman. Having stated this, I believe you'll understand why coming in second is not an option and why my petty torments forced me to change the playing field. I took on a pawn; his name, Jared Dean Statner. His occupation: midnight DJ for the local radio station KTOP. His call sign: JD. In gratitude, he sent me the following reenactment of our sexual power play.

Spun

I pushed through the door into my office and locked it behind me. Taking a seat behind my console, I turned on the table light and stared somberly at the microphone. I had always regarded myself as a perfectionist when it came to my work, but now I spent my days haunted by the man I used to be.

During the day I attempted to prepare new material that would gain listeners, yet my ideas regrettably reflected my imperfections. I needed the midnight slot to take top ratings, just once, so I could prove to the boss (that rat bastard) that I should be given my morning show back. I hadn't deserved the demotion I'd received.

It shouldn't have been a big deal, my girlfriend relishing me with a blowjob in the movie theater. Yet that conniving tabloid piranha snapped those incriminating pictures with his cell phone. And Charles, my boss, who *never* did anything wrong, had made certain that my flourishing career ended because of the incident.

Everyone had something to say about my little indiscretion: the cops, the newspapers, and especially the station manager. The whole ordeal went front page: "Noted Disc Jockey Caught Having Sex in Movie Theater." What a fiasco. Even though no formal charges were filed, the damage had been done.

Sulking, I pulled out the CD changer, filled it, then walked into the back room and turned on the coffee machine. "No job is worth this humiliation," I said, staring back at my seat. For eight years, I had held top ratings for the morning time slot; now I was lucky if thirty people tuned in.

I grabbed a cup of coffee, returned to my desk, and lit up my stage. As the red light faded to green, I began, "By the look of the night lights, only the partying night-owls are still awake out there. If that's true, pick up the phone and let me know what you think about sex. The topic's open."

I stared down at the phone lines—only three lit up. I picked up line one. "You're on the air."

"JD, my man. How's it going?"

"You really want to know?"

"Listen man, you used to be so cool. My girl and I tuned into the morning show all the time, but now you suck!"

Quickly, I disconnected the line. Line two. "Caller, you're on the air."

"Yo, JD, before you hang up on me, I have an idea how to get your morning slot back."

Intrigued, I replied, "How's that?"

"Get up and unlock the door."

"Do what?"

"Just go. Let the lady in to do *her* job."

The phone line went dead. "I'll be right back listeners," I said into the microphone as I realized that I had nothing to lose, and got up and unlocked the door.

A tall and statuesque woman, wearing a long black trench coat and six-inch stiletto heels materialized. "Holy shit," I sputtered, backing away from her.

"Hello," she murmured. She sauntered towards me, stopping less than two feet from my reach, then dropped her coat and revealed her naked form.

Her perfect body bedazzled me and I exhaled a long deep sigh. The woman's legs were long and lean. Magnificently chiseled, they seemed to go on forever, rising up to greet her well-defined thighs. Her thighs curved in to meet her heart-shaped patch of curls, her sexual hood graciously budding outward, beckoning me. Mesmerized, my gaze traveled up, discovering the rest of her luscious body. Her waist arced in, tightly caressing her ribs. Her breasts were full, firm, and what I estimated to be at least a full C cup. Her nipples jutted out, perky and alert, tempting me to take them into my mouth. My lust awakened, my appetite whetted and I panted, "My God, your body is truly awe-inspiring."

Unclad, she sidled towards me, closer and closer until her breath heated my neck. "Thanks for letting me in," she whispered.

Enthralled, I took her face between my hands and drew her towards me. My lips touched hers. Her mouth opened. Our tongues met in a dueling caress.

The warmth of her tongue prompted a sensation that spread through me like lightning. My arousal grew and my breath caught when she placed her hands on my shoulders and lightly traced my back through my shirt, then finally rested them on my ass and squeezed tightly. I bit down gently on her bottom lip, savoring the tender morsel.

"Oh yeah," she moaned, inviting more aggression.

Capturing her hair in my hands, I tugged on it playfully. Her burnished red locks glowed like fire against her defenseless tan skin. Her body bore no tan lines, so either she had naturally dark skin, or she spent hours tanning in the nude. I opted for a tanning-bed scenario. I pictured her lying naked, headphones on, listening to music, basking in the heat that surrounded her. I imagined her hands tracing the length of her body, purposefully landing between her legs, her fingers sliding between her slick folds and slipping into her warm, moist, bed of desire.

A searing pain against my lip drew me out of my revere as she bit me wantonly. I licked my lip to pamper my injury. She began unbuttoning my shirt, then pushed it off my shoulders and watched it fall to the ground. Her skill at unbuttoning my jeans proved without a doubt that she had done this before. After the top button gave way, she pulled on my pants, smirking as the rest of the buttons popped open. Her forcefulness, a delightful surprise.

Clothed only in boxers, the naked proof of my manhood failed to stay within its cotton constraints. "Who are you?" I gasped.

Slyly deflecting my question, she reached down and traced the length of my engorged member with her nails. I nibbled on her neck, and then tenderly pushed her shoulders down, forcing her to the floor. Once on her knees, she took hold of my boxers and slowly pulled them down, inch by inch, teasing me. As she pulled, she kissed every inch my newly bared flesh, panting moistly. Her tongue followed the enticing kisses, tickling me.

Once my dick emerged, she sucked me into her mouth, the warmth of which forced me to moan aloud, "Oh fuck yeah. Keep sucking that cock."

Her skilled tongue tortured me, first licking the ultra-sensitive tip of my shaft, then running down to the end of my dick and back up. She sucked me hard, forcing my cock to leak the pre-cum of my inevitable release. She didn't seem to mind the salty sweet taste of my passion. Positioning her hand around my pulsing length, squeezing and stroking, she kept her mouth securely around it at all times. Her tongue tickled, her lips suckled, and her hands never left my flesh.

Exhaling a heated breath, I thought that the foreplay couldn't get better. I writhed under her magical touch, my passion heightening. Still, I pulled her head away from my turgid girth and knelt down on the floor as she lay back and her knees fell wide open, engaging my attention. "Oh baby, stay still and let me taste your sweetness," I begged, gazing animalistically at her passion-swollen lips.

Slowly I inched forward, kissing one knee, then the other. Impatiently I slid my tongue up her inner thigh until I reached her source of womanly desire. Tauntingly, I bypassed her heavenly gate, running my tongue down her other thigh. Once my tongue met her knee, I lifted first one leg, then the other up over my shoulders. Quickly I returned my lithe tongue to her wanting bed of delight, searching her sex, sucking upon it greedily. Then I slid one finger into her moist, heated shell and played. While my fingers and tongue were simultaneously devouring her, I resolutely and energetically rubbed my face on her thighs.

She moaned and squirmed beneath me, her satiny bulb growing moister with every flick of my tongue, until finally her body tensed and she started to climax. I lifted my face from between her legs and positioned myself to take her. Inserting the tip of my dick against her flesh, I entered her in one slow push, becoming one with her body. I moaned huskily as I moved, twisted, and maneuvered my body to fill her. Her body forcefully met my every move, her tits bouncing.

I hoisted her up so she sat on my lap. "Fuck me...fuck me hard...pinch my nipples!" she yelled. Her juices flowed, warming my cock. The sounds of slapping bodies and of me spanking her bottom filled the air. Our moans and cries drowned one another out as our mutual satisfaction exploded in a sheen of sweat.

As our breathing quieted, I realized that I had never turned off my microphone. "Damn, we were on the air!" I sputtered, jumping up to rectify the situation.

"Okay, listeners, you've just experienced what we like to call role-playing. Call in and let me know if we were really having sex or not. After a brief weather update, I'll open the lines."

Instantly, all the lines lit up. In addition, my private line began to flash. I hesitated before picking it up, knowing my boss was on the other end. "Hello. Yes, sir."

Without haste, the goddess situated next to me grabbed the phone out of my hand and covered the mouthpiece. "Is your boss giving you a bad time?" she inquired.

"Well, you could say that."

"Let me help you," she replied, and then raised the phone to speak.

"Charles?" she asked. "I think you know who this is. Listen, if you don't want your wife to find out about your little late-night rendezvous with me, you'll hear me out. JD gets the morning slot back, and this little incident is explained as a magnificent stunt. There's no negotiation. JD knows everything." She said nothing more, as if listening to his reply. Then grinning wickedly, she hung up the phone.

I snatched the sublime woman next to me about the waist and pulled her to me, kissing her feverishly on the mouth. My tongue danced with hers, showing my appreciation. After I let her go, she picked up her coat, slipped on her shoes, handed me a piece of paper, then turned and left the room.

I looked at the paper she had given me: her number, her address, and 8 A.M. were the only information written on it. I tucked it safely into my pocket and turned the microphone back on. After a sigh of relief, I announced with great pleasure, "We have the final tally from the audience and I'm happy to say that thanks to you listeners, the midnight DJ is signing off."

CHAPTER 6

The best thing that could have ever happened was Charles's emotional defection from me. I found myself craving a new way of life. I am a sexual being by nature and the need to fulfill my urges must be appeased. I set out to take a break from "older gentlemen" and the power they exude, by capturing an arrogant young stockbroker. We both enjoyed a passion for movies, which led us quickly to the comforts of his home movie theater. Together we spent a glorious weekend critiquing the sexual displays of actors, as well as our own, more fundamental actions. The creative and ingenious performance I used to master John would have led any actress down the red carpet for the Oscar.

Intermission

I gave a heavy sigh of tedium when John hit slow motion on the controls and Demi Moore unleashed her passion upon Michael Douglas once again. "How many times are we going to watch this scene?" I inquired tired of the actors in "Disclosure." Deviously I knew that I wanted to *disclose* something of my own.

"Until I'm satisfied," he muttered in response.

"Can I get you something?" I asked.

Receiving only a vague shrug in response, I went to the kitchen. My thoughts were jumbled. I didn't want food. I wanted John hot for me. I wanted my man. Also, I wanted something that could be equally enjoyed and consumed by us both. My mind reminisced, revisiting a recent sexual experiment with ice-cream toppings and our mutual sweet tooth.

Opening the fridge, I spied several leftover delectable toppings: caramel, fudge, whipped cream, all extremely flesh-worthy. I eyed the lonely bananas on the counter waiting patiently to be sucked on or dipped into my hidden treasures. My imagination ran wild envisioning ways to entice John into the kitchen. I didn't need him to supply creative inspiration; I just wanted his body to pleasure mine. Yet before I had a chance to coerce him into the kitchen, I felt his fingers toying with my hair. Silent as a stalking tiger, he had snuck up behind me.

"Missed you on the sofa," he said.

"I thought I told you that I needed to be satisfied," I replied. "And quite frankly, Demi isn't doing it for me. With that in mind I decided to go straight for the temptations of dessert." Putting my hands on the counter, I hoisted myself up.

"Well, who is dessert first?" John asked playfully. "By the looks of where I caught you, you were planning on starting without me."

"On the contrary," I stated.

I watched as John opened the freezer door, pulled out an ice-cube tray, and set it down on the counter. Then he opened the fridge, took out the caramel, fudge and whipped cream, and set them all in a row on the counter.

"Eenie, meenie, miny, moe, catch a flavor by its toe," he began to chant. His fingers lingered momentarily on each item, until finally coming to rest on the ice cubes.

Quickly, John shimmied out of his shirt and shorts, exposing his silken shaft. His erection jutted out from the junction of his thighs: hot, hard, and raring to go. Eagerly, he grabbed a couple ice cubes and rubbed them on himself, apparently attempting to ease his maddening desire. It didn't work. His cock stood at attention.

I watched intensely as the ice melted over his erection with every stroke of his hand. Envious of his playtime, I stripped out of my thin cotton dress. Once naked, I let my fingernails trace the outline of the other ice cubes. "What are you planning on doing with these?" I inquired provocatively.

John's eyes sparkled with mischief. "What's it to you?"

I ached for release. Not with the ice, but with John. I wanted him to thrust into my warm flesh and impel me to the pinnacle of sexual satisfaction. I reached down and teased the tip of his mushroom-capped shaft with my finger. "You seem to have sprung a leak," I said, circling the tip of his mounting erection. His eyes widened as he watched me raise my glistening finger to my mouth and lick it clean.

John grabbed an ice cube and smoothed it across my neck. His eyes devoured me, following the movement of the cold cube down my body. My labored breathing became short gasps as he encircled my nipples in icy pleasure. I moaned, anticipating the trail the ice would take as it trickled down between my passion-swollen lips.

John seized another cube from the rapidly dwindling supply. He followed the chilled path with the heat of his tongue, seeming to delight in my uncontrollable shivers. I squirmed beneath his onslaught as he slid a cube between my pulsing lips. Teasingly he circled the tight bud of my rapture, and then penetrated my flesh. Impelling the ice further into me, he plundered my treasure chest of infinite delight, while his long, agile fingers provided the friction my wildly heaving body craved.

I prompted John to follow the course the melting ice had taken with his mouth as well as his fingers. Placing my hands on his head I pushed him towards the center of my passion. He buried his face in the cradle of my thighs. His tongue lightly caressed my wanting bed of delight. Then he closed his lips around the tender tip of my need, leisurely sucking at the same time that his tongue skillfully circled, engulfing the sweet nectar of my flavor. My begging moans became un-muffled cries of lustful need, "Please. Please. Oh that's it. Oh yeah. Fuck John, I can't stand any more."

Ignoring my plea, he thrust his lissome tongue into my cleft, forcing the frozen chip to melt under the heat of his willing whipping. My back arched and my hips thrust forward. No muzzle could've hindered my vivacious voice as my muscles clenched around his tongue in rhythmic spasms and I screamed in pleasure, "Oh God, I'm coming. I'm coming. I'm coming!"

When I finally regained my breath, I was pleased to see how John's body had reacted to my outward acknowledgment of his oral mastery. As my muscles relaxed and my eyes opened fully, he met my look with a ravenous stare. Smiling, I reached out and picked the caramel off the counter, declaring throatily, "Now it's your turn, John. I pray to God you're ready."

Preparing to accost him, I slid off the counter, then inched my way down his exposed thigh. I slowly twisted the top off the caramel, dipped my fingers into the sticky sweet topping, and knelt on the floor between John's athletic legs. Forcefully pushing him against the counter, I commanded, "Lean back, big boy, you're gonna need the support."

John froze when I took hold of his rock-hard erection. I slid my hand down to the base of his scrotum where I began massaging him. With my other hand I began smearing the gooey caramel from the top of his dick down to his heavy, clean-shaven balls. "I've always loved the taste of caramel," I cooed, nibbling the tip of his erect cock.

I savored the process of licking each and every ridge of his pulsing dick, and once his shaft had been shined I reached for the whipped cream. John's eyes clenched shut when I replaced my moist, hot mouth with a burst of cold confection. Deep moans escaped his tensed jaws as I wrapped my mouth around him, once again attempting to swallow his manhood whole. John couldn't help but gyrate faster as I engulfed him. He moved from an erotic dance to full undulating thrusts within moments, letting go completely.

My mouth left his cock and as my tongue slid across his balls never letting my stroke idle. My hand glided rhythmically up and down the length of him, while I continued to torture his balls within the enclosure of my heated mouth. John's sensitive sack shifted with each stroke of my tongue. My pace quickened, faster and faster. His rock-hard pecker oozed excitement. I felt the life force within him being uprooted, and voraciously I sucked it out of him. Out of control, he could no longer hold back. He pulled my mouth away, forcing me to arch back, just as his cock erupted violently onto my beautiful upraised breasts in a string of luminous pearls.

When all his desire had been unleashed, I smiled. Admiring the sticky fluid coating my breasts I said, "The Oscars might not approve of our performance, but I believe Hugh Heffner certainly would."

CHAPTER 7

One summer, my grandmother was in need of my assistance after surgery, so I dropped everything to help her. I chose a vacation rental near my grandparent's home in order to retain my freedom, yet still be close enough to provide comfort.

Being from out of town, I didn't have any connections to the dating scene, but I wanted to see the sights and enjoy some carefree companionship. My grandmother instructed me to take advantage of the video dating service her best friend's daughter owned. Once my grandmother was safe at home after her procedure, I took her advice and went into town to make "my movie." Never underestimate the seductive power of one who makes love to the camera.

Dating Demo

I disrobed as I went up the stairs. Hurriedly pulling my tank top over my head, I let out a heavy sigh when my distended nipples caught the edge of my top. My stomach fluttered as I imagined my date laying a hot trail across my bare breasts with his lips. Kyle's video had captivated me. I had watched like a starved cat ready to pounce, a feral sexual predator, as his steely blue eyes stared through the camera, piercing my soul. His name flowed easily from my mouth. "Kyle—now that's a name I can scream in the throes of passion."

I surveyed my reflection in the mirror, and a tingle surged between my thighs, electrifying my senses. I could feel my juices stirring. If I didn't get into the shower quickly, I'd start taking matters into my *own* hands. Besides, even though I'd left the door unlocked for him with instructions to make himself at home, I didn't want to keep him waiting for too long.

Still filled with desire, I rubbed my hands over my body, gently massaged the silken tips of my nipples, and then glided down to the moistening, warm folds of my sex. I stepped into the shower and embraced the water's warm caress. My restless hunger summoned me to action but I knew I couldn't waste my sexual need on myself, so I quickly showered and got out.

I walked to the bed and retrieved my undergarments, goose-bumps adorning my damp flesh. I pulled my scarlet bra and matching panties over my voluptuous curves, and savored the feeling of the silky fabric easing over my skin. I paused briefly, relishing the thought of Kyle stripping my decorated flesh. Enthusiastically, I shimmied into the red mini-dress I'd chosen for the night's delights. Sitting down at the vanity, I dried my hair and carefully applied my makeup. The finished product that stared back at me from the mirror reflected that I *was* ready for the evening's proceedings. I rose swiftly, slipped on my clogs and glided back down the stairwell, alight with dreamy thoughts of the night's unknown enchantments.

I inhaled the rich smoky aroma of a wood fire as I neared the sunken living room. "I love a man who can set the scene for romance," I murmured, sauntering through the archway, scanning for my welcome interloper. My first glance took in a bottle of wine and two exquisite silver goblets situated perfectly beside a bouquet of flowers on the mantle. Smiling, I surveyed the room until I found myself captured in Kyle's molten gaze.

"The matches were on the mantle. I hope you don't mind?" he said with a twinkle of mischief in his eye.

His deep rich voice enticed me toward him, "Not at all," I replied.

As Kyle poured us both goblets of claret Merlot, his eyes swept appreciatively over my silhouette. I swirled my wine.

"Your beauty is more intoxicating than the wine," he said huskily, as he lifted his goblet to salute me. "Madam, I'm at your mercy."

I decided to make my toast direct and to the point and lifted my goblet to him. "To mutual enjoyment and a fulfilling evening."

"Sounds promising," Kyle purred.

Realizing that we had not yet made proper introductions, I said, "Well Kyle, you know my name, my likes and dislikes, but is there *anything* you want to know that wasn't on the tape?"

Kyle's lips curved in a sensual smile. "Now that you ask, just how far will you go on the first date?"

"All depends on how good a dancer he is. I mean, can he seduce me further than just a whimsical twirl and a simple kiss?"

Kyle's eyes darkened, his pupils flaring with apparent lust. He retrieved a flower from the vase on the mantel and approached me, bringing the fragrant bud to my cheek, and then trailing it downward towards my aching breasts.

I inhaled the heady scent of rose petal and quivered, as the flower's progression over my body became intimate. My breath caught when Kyle dipped the flower between my breasts. When he raised the bud back up, he traced the outline of my lips with the velvety petals. Instantly, I was overcome as a wave of pleasure, dark and drugged, washed over me.

Adrenalin coursed through my veins. I reached down to retrieve the stereo remote and push the play button. My hips began to sway to the haunting beat of Enigma's "Principles of Lust." When Kyle opened his arms to me, mesmerized, I floated into his embrace. Together we shared perfect rhythm.

We danced slowly, seductively, around the room. Kyle's hands roamed relentlessly, caressing, fondling each curve and hollow of my body. When his hands cupped my firm buttocks he pulled me close, and I felt his steely hardness pulsing through my flimsy clothing. "God I want you," he breathed raspily into my ear. "But I'll stop…I swear…unless you give me the go-ahead."

The blatant need in Kyle's declaration prompted my cry of hedonistic longing. "Take me—ravage me—make me scream!"

As the words left my lips, Kyle grabbed me with his strong hands and bent me forward over the arm of the sofa. He grasped the hemline of my dress and hoisted it upward over my ass. Before I could move, Kyle had seized my waist, pulled my thong over my hips and to the floor, then sensually pressed his immense arousal against me. I listened with a hint of apprehension as his zipper gave way. His sex flexed against my bare buttocks, searching, begging entry.

His cock was long and one of the thickest I had ever encountered. My body instinctively flinched in sexual frenzy as Kyle maneuvered himself into my tight sheath, slowly penetrating me, like a key easing into a well-oiled lock. My moans voiced both pleasure and slight pain. His first full thrust left me hazy with passion. As he sank his steel shaft fully within my liquid glide, I met his every thrust, pressing back forcefully against his huge dick, impelling him deeper into my moist, quivering and contracting cove. I quickly became aware that Kyle could be my sexual equal and I relished the idea of the sensual pleasure still to come.

Reaching back, I took hold of Kyle's ass. When I turned my head to the side, my eyes caught his, and I begged him, without words, to slow down so I could shift positions. As his motions idled, I turned my body over, moving one leg, then the other, until my legs wrapped around his waist. Then I crossed my ankles and clenched my ass tight, which forced my velvety depths to contract around his pulsing, thick rod.

I dropped my arms back above my head, grabbed onto the sofa cushion and pumped my pelvis forward, meeting his every undulating thrust. I felt he was close to climaxing, so I reached back up and clamped onto his toned ass, pulled it close, refusing to let him go until he gave into his need. The ravenous hunger he had created within me ached for release. "Fuck me, Kyle! Fuck me good!" I screamed in wild ecstasy.

No sooner had these words escaped my lips than I felt Kyle explode within me. His body shook with unbridled convulsions. I held tight to his firm ass, clasping his cock deep within my pulsing walls.

Kyle didn't move. He kept his head buried in my shoulder and his cock inside my tight shell. Once his breathing slowed he collapsed over onto the couch and pulled me to join him. "What's left for our second date?" he asked, as he swept my hair up in his hands and kissed my neck.

I did not reply until he rose from the couch, drew me up into his arms and headed toward the stairway. As we neared the stairwell, I looked at him smiling, and replied in my best Scarlet O'Hara, "Frankly, my dear Kyle...I don't give a damn."

CHAPTER 8

In this technological era of computers and e-mail, one can never be sure what kind of correspondence one will receive and from whom. The following is rewritten in the style of an email I received from Josh, a friend to those in need. His recollection of our hiatus will surely shed light on the kindness of strangers.

Having traveled extensively, I decided some time ago to lose my inhibition surrounding public nudity. One summer I chose to vacation at a resort that had access to a local nudist beach. Don't get me wrong, I have a voracious appetite for sex, and love to be naked, but I am not a public exhibitionist. After check-in, I decided to try the nearby beach for a swim. I left my room clad only in my whimsical "Carmen San Diego" trench coat.

With the sun beating down on me, I happily discarded my covering once I stepped onto the sandy beach. My nakedness enlivened my senses. I became aroused as the silken waters caressed my bared flesh. I was lost in enjoyment when the sky grew dark and rain began to fall.

When I finally left the water my newly energized outlook on life led me to do the unthinkable. I went to the door and peered in the window of a small house like a voyeur. An extremely handsome man lay on the couch sleeping, alone, waiting for me to devour him.

The Good Samaritan

Dear Lady of the Rain,
    It hadn't rained in a month and what started as a light drizzle became a torrential downpour as I settled into the couch. Today was the type of day where a good book

and a hot beverage made everything complete. I set down my coffee mug, closed my eyes, and eased into the waiting arms of Morpheus.

The persistent summons of the doorbell disrupted my slumber and jolted me from my prone position. I staggered toward the front door and saw the profile of a woman standing on my front porch. I took the doorknob in hand and cautiously opened the door to see her more clearly. Obviously she'd been caught in the weather unprepared. Droplets of water dripped off the ends of her hair and before I had a chance to say anything the woman turned to face me.

I wiped the sleep from my eyes and was taken aback by her stunning good looks. She appeared to be in her midtwenties and had blue eyes the color of a tropical ocean. Her slicked-back long dark hair lay halfway down her back and she stood about five foot six. The smile across her face as she stared back at me implied that she liked what she saw. Utterly captivated, I asked, "Can I help you?"

The stranger gently nudged past me, and entered the house. Once inside, she turned to face me and uttered one word, "Towel."

For a moment I couldn't move. I stood in the doorway, jaw wide open. Her audacity caught me off guard. Surprised and strangely aroused, my growing hard-on compelled me to accede to her request and I walked over to the linen closet.

I felt the woman inch up behind me as I rustled through the cupboard. The warmth of her breath caressed my ear and neck. I was stunned by her closeness. Cautiously I turned around, holding a soft maroon towel. With a coyly raised brow she took the towel from me and began to dry her hair.

I felt extremely vulnerable, lost in her beauty, her confidence and her sexuality. Her body, only inches from mine, proved too tempting to resist. Unconsciously I placed my hands on hers and together, in perfect rhythm, we began to dry her wet tresses with the towel. After only a few moments, she slowly dropped one hand to her side, then the other. I continued to dry her hair with one hand while shifting the other to begin unbuttoning her wet overcoat.

Starting with the top button, I worked my way down. She didn't move, nor did she try to stop me. Instead she locked eyes with me briefly, then tilted her head back and closed her lids. I sensed she wanted to lose herself in the moment; so gradually, slowly, teasingly, I continued to unbutton her coat. When the fourth and last button loosened, the slope of her breasts came into view.

Dedicating myself to the task of disrobing her completely, I took my other hand off her head. The towel fell in a clump on the floor behind her. Now with both my hands free, I slid them inside her coat and gently rubbed her soft damp skin.

When my hands came to rest at the small of her back, her overcoat parted, granting me access to all her glory. Not a stitch of clothing veiled her body under the rain doused material. Her phenomenal tanned curves provoked me to wet my suddenly dry mouth and lick my lips with erotic expectation. I pushed the fabric over her shoulders, allowing it to fall on the floor in a sodden mass next to the towel. I stared lingeringly, soaking in her beauty until my willpower gave way to lust and I pulled her to me in a desperate embrace.

My lips met hers; I tasted the trickling remnants of the storm and we became one. Our tongues interlaced, dancing inside each other's mouth. This kiss filled me with energy, restlessness, and excitement. The pace of our breathing increased as our tongues forged on in frenzied hunger.

Pausing briefly, I cupped her face in my hands and inhaled her evocative perfume. Then, beginning at the base of her neck, I teased her flesh, commencing my exploration of her body. First little licks, then gentle nibbles, until finally she gasped, alerting me to the right path. I needed to devour her, body and soul. Urgently I hastened my search to find every secret erogenous zone of her body, inching downward until my attention converged upon her bountiful breasts.

I revere women's breasts, especially their areolas and nipples. Her nipples puckered with desire, reaching out, demanding my affection. They were so beautiful and irresistible that I kissed the tops of them. Then I nibbled, providing a gentle friction as I pulled each one individually into my mouth.

Unexpectedly, she threaded her fingers through my hair and pulled taut, forcing my head downward. Suddenly I found myself kneeling on the floor before her, and she vigorously pressed my head between her legs. My mouth seized the treasure hidden between her thighs and brushed against her soft tight curls. My talented tongue tasted her outer lips and my fingers opened her and fondled her purposefully. Her sensual juices flowed with each flick of my tongue and thrust of my finger.

The nub of her pleasure developed a pulse of its own and she squirmed uncontrollably under my darting tongue and moist suction. Her nails dug lightly into my scalp. My jeans bound my stiff rod; I needed to discard them, to begin to ease my torment. I wanted to please her, but as I halted my advances in order to free myself, she pulled me to my feet.

Once I was standing she began unbuttoning my 501 jeans. The last silver button popped free; she slid her hand into the opening and found my engorged length. She flashed a wicked smile, dropped to her knees before me and dragged my jeans down to the floor with her. My rock hard dick sprang into full view. She grabbed tightly onto me, sliding her hand up and down the expanse of my thick shaft. Then she tasted her way from the base of my dick to the tip, encasing me fully within her mouth, licking me, sucking me, and teasing me, first hard, then soft.

My ass tightened, and my body arched, about to explode, as she glided her tongue along the rim of my throbbing trunk. This was by far the best blowjob I had ever received. Although exulting in the oral pleasure she gave me, I desired more. I needed the feverish heat of her sex closing tightly around my cock. Hastily I lifted her and placed her back firmly against the wall. I grabbed my dick and positioned it against the portal of her passion, then, moaning, I savored the feeling of penetration. This still wasn't enough.

Yearning to dominate her body, I lowered her to the floor and climbed atop. Her body gyrated underneath me, and as her ass contracted, she heaved upward with each of my thrusts. I pulled her legs around my neck. Her tits bounced before me. I knew her orgasm was close when she screamed, louder and louder, "Yes…yes…oh God yes!"

With each scream, I plunged faster and harder. Thrusting in, searing her, pulling out, harder and harder, deeper and deeper, I continued until my cock exploded within her quivering flesh. Her body shook as her climax ended and her inner muscles milked me dry with their clenching grip.

I couldn't help but collapse on top of her. Unable to move after my magnificent orgasm, I lay with her, saying nothing. The pleasure of her had exhausted me beyond repair, and I held her close for a moment before passing out in ecstasy.

I was roused from my slumber by the ringing of the phone. I reluctantly got up off the floor and answered it.

"Hello."

"Hi, honey, how are you?" my wife inquired from the other end.

"Ah...fine," I murmured.

"Well, what have you been up to on this rainy day?"

"Nothing much. Just dreaming of wild sex," I replied. But when I turned around, surveying my surroundings, my jaw fell open. On the floor by the linen closet lay a wet maroon towel.

"Honey, let me call you right back."

I knew the moment I set the phone back in its cradle that I had to contact you, *My Lady of the Rain*. Thank you for leaving your e-mail address for me. Married or not, it honored me to be able to help you out of the downpour; to be your Good Samaritan in your time of need.

With all my admiration,
Josh

CHAPTER 9

To pamper myself, I spend one evening a week submerged in the bathtub, reading erotic literature as bubbles tickle my flesh and candles flicker all around me. It was during one of these nights that I came across a strangely familiar story in the form of a letter, which propelled me to reminisce about my flight of fancy with Todd in California.

One beautiful, sunny summer afternoon we met by chance and spent a glorious day together. It started as I was leaning under the hood of my broken-down jeep. Todd's wrong turn onto "my" highway led him to rescue me. Our paths crossed and we paved our own road that afternoon.

I smiled, knowing all too well that the author's tale was true, even though he had submitted it as a work of fiction to the magazine. I giggled when I realized that he had turned our afternoon of sexual exploration into an eloquent piece of literature, and although the names had been changed, the events and pleasures were accurately portrayed. I am thankful to have stumbled across Todd's work of "fiction" and am elated to share it with you.

Hog Wild

Todd pulled his hair back and tied it tight under a yellow bandana before he left the city early that morning. A quick ride turned into a long journey on the open road. He left the house a little before eight, wearing jeans, a white T-shirt, a brown leather vest and his black boots; attire that might be deemed inappropriate for fine dining. But fine dining would prove to be precisely what lay in store for him.

A wrong turn onto Highway 101 led him to an empty stretch of road. The sweltering California sun beat down relentlessly; it seemed to melt the road, forming mirages. But the lifted hood on a bright yellow jeep was quite real.

The roar of his Harley's motor quieted as he pulled over to see if he could help. Who could enjoy a beautiful summer day stranded on the side of the road? He killed the engine and parked his bike behind the jeep. Once he came close enough to touch the driver's side door, he understood why luck led him to take this unexpected route.

His eyes traced the length of the woman's body. He took inventory, starting with her scarlet cowboy boots. God! They looked hot against the deep golden sheen of her skin. He stood motionless, riveted by her beauty as she bent over to retrieve what appeared to be her radiator cap. Her athletically sculpted thighs curved up into her luscious round ass, her faded cut-offs tantalizingly exposing the curve of her buttocks.

"Thank you, God," Todd sighed, shifting uncomfortably, feeling suddenly stifled within the tight fit of his own well-worn denim.

The stranded desert goddess turned to face him, the tendrils of her seductively short chestnut curls clung to her sweat-moistened brow. Small triangles of light cotton barely covered her taut brown nipples, where beads of sweat formed in the valley between her voluptuous breasts. "My bandana would cover more of her breasts than that top," he thought.

Realizing she had an observer, she pulled her sunglasses down over her nose in order to see him better. Gathering her thick cap of hair between her fingers, she carelessly tousled it, cooling her scalp. As if reading his thoughts, she trailed her fingers over the slope of her breasts in order to follow her handsome suitor's lustful gaze. "Damn hot out here, isn't it?" she inquired throatily, extending her hand. "My name's Sophie."

He captured her hand and stroked her inner palm with his index finger. Clearing his throat he replied, "Todd."

She laughed uninhibitedly, seeming pleased with his bold, teasing caress.

"Anything I can help you with?" he offered, releasing her hand.

She nodded. "Well, the tow truck's on its way, but I'd sure like a ride to town. Besides, it's been a long time since I've had a powerful machine between my thighs."

Without a doubt, Todd knew that Sophie usually got exactly what she wanted. "Well then, hop on," he replied, spinning around and striding back to his bike. He turned it over, revved the gas and inched forward towards her. Like a gentleman, he extended his hand to help her on, but unaided she threw her leg over the bike. Sophie hugged him tightly around the waist, leaned forward and breathed into his ear, "Harleys are an incredible turn-on for me."

Todd dropped his hand to her leg and slid it along her bare thigh until he reached her ass. "*You're* an incredible turn-on for me," he said, as they took off. With his hand on her ass, he traced under the frayed edge of her cutoffs, sliding his fingers across the smooth flesh beneath. It didn't take long for him to realize that she wore no panties. Intrigued, he tucked his fingers into the crevice between her rounded cheeks, wishing silently that she was sitting in front of him so he could explore her damp recess.

Todd squirmed as Sophie slid her hands from his waist to his knees, massaging her way up his muscled inner thighs, pausing when she reached his strained juncture. His breath caught as her inquisitive finger wiggled into his jeans between the buttons and began teasing him with abandon. He laughed, knowing that her fingers met with his bare skin. He loved being naked beneath his jeans, for it allowed his cock breathing room. Tired of teasing Sophie took both hands, pulled open the buttons on his jeans and unleashed his fiercely growing manhood.

Only one word came to Todd's mind to describe her: incredible. His impatience peaked. He wanted to consume her. Hungrily he reached down, took her hand and raised it to his mouth. He tasted the tip of her finger before sucking it, attempting to torture her senses with the succulent heat of his moist tongue. One by one, he drew her fingers into his mouth, lubricating them with his saliva, erotically savoring all of her delicate digits, before lowering her newly moistened slick hand back to his swollen, exposed flesh.

Sophie tightened her fingers around his girth and began gliding her hand up and down. Todd put his hand to hers and aided her in her motions. He kept her close to the tip of his dick, where he squeezed her hand, encouraging her to fondle his most sensitive area. He knew she was getting impatient when she let go of his rock-hard flesh, leaned back and raised her legs up around his waist, carefully locking her ankles together while she talentedly unbuttoned her cutoffs. Once her shorts were loosened her legs returned to the passenger pegs and she leaned her chest in to him. He felt her one hand press against his ass as it slid against her flesh, while the other returned to hold his member.

Todd imagined the feat at hand as she sat behind him masturbating. He wished that he could be a participant instead of only the driver. He didn't want to concentrate on the road and keeping the bike under control, he wanted to dominate her flesh. He felt her hand begin to move frantically against his ass, and he envisioned her massaging her satiny bulb. Her motions became fast and furious as her fingers again tightened on his extended length. With each contraction she squeezed his dick harder and it swelled, his veins forming ridges engorged with blood. Feeling his enthusiasm, she screamed out to the winds, tightening her hand in maddening spasms around his distended cock as she came, "Oh fuck! I wish you were inside me right now!" When her orgasm ended, she moved her freed hand forward, grabbing his balls.

He could smell her natural perfume flowing up to him as she used her own lubrication to pleasure him. The hum of the bike's motor and each vibration of the road aided her in her venture. Over and over she tightened her hand, convulsively pumping his throbbing organ until he exploded. Milking his remaining essence, she pulled the bandana from his head and polished the length of his spent flesh.

Reveling in Sophie's inventiveness, he beamed. Suddenly, out of nowhere, a road sign indicated a nearby camping area. Todd turned immediately onto the small dirt road and followed the arrows.

Sophie leaned forward and purred, "Where we headed?"

He lifted her hand to his lips, kissed her palm and replied, "Somewhere I can pleasure you comfortably."

"Hurry," she moaned excitedly.

Within minutes, a beautiful lake surrounded by trees and rolling grassland came into view. Todd pulled into a parking spot and killed the engine. He watched as Sophie swung her leg over and hopped off the bike without refastening her buttons. Todd looked around; perfect—just like Eden—not a soul in sight. He rummaged through the saddlebags and retrieved a thick Navajo blanket.

With a bemused expression on her face, Sophie laughingly asked, "Do you always come so readily prepared?"

"Never know what kind of trouble I might run into," he retorted.

"Now I'm trouble, huh?"

"That's for damn sure."

Todd wished he had a camera. Sophie looked fabulous, her form the embodiment of a teenage boy's lurid daydreams. He watched as she reached back and untied her top with slow deliberate motions. Once free, her large breasts jiggled as she gave a slight shimmy. Then she wiggled her hips in a provocative striptease, releasing her shorts to their place on the ground. His gaze fastened on the crisp curls between her sun-kissed thighs.

Todd's breath caught in his throat. No longer did she look just fabulous…she was perfect! Her petite delectable frame seemed almost overshadowed by her voluptuous breasts. The provocative promise her nubile figure offered forced Todd's eyes to glaze over with lust when Sophie licked her lips with delight. "Goddamn! *Playboy* missed a perfect centerfold!" he exclaimed. He could tell she enjoyed the effect she had on him, and this increased his desire to bury himself deep within her.

Sophie smirked, and reaching down, pulled her right boot off by the heel. Then slowly she did the same with the left. Both boots off, she walked toward the water, placed first one foot in the lake, then the other. She must have felt his eyes making love to her, for she turned and waved him over. Then coyly, she walked further out, the water hiding her perfect form from his view.

Todd met the water's edge just as Sophie's head went below the surface. When she came up for air he was standing naked. Gradually he moved towards her. With each of his strides, the water lapped up a little higher on her body. Tiny waves crested against her breasts, promising to reach up to her neck. When he reached her and they stood face to face, the waters calmed and their passions were swept into turmoil.

Sophie's hands grazed over the light dusting of hair across his muscled chest. A shiver raced through his body with each pass of her fingertips, leaving a frenzied hunger in their trail.

Todd felt he could no longer wait to possess her; he wanted to master her with the primitive heat of his lust. Snatching her around the waist, he hoisted her high up out of the water, feasting his eyes on her exposed body. As he gradually brought her back down, he nibbled her tender flesh, his lips lingering on her tanned skin. She wrapped her legs around his body, nudging the entry to her private Eden against his rigid length.

Tortured by the wait, Todd's cock flexed against her, begging entrance. His hand slid down and found her semiparted lips. He teased the outer edge of her silken glide with his fingers, inserting one, then another, simultaneously taking them out, and then replacing them again in her fluid channel. He felt her body's moist heat flow as her tender flesh softened around his searching fingers. His wait proved well worth it, for when he entered her, he slid in snugly. Her blazing folds encased him, closing in a velvet clasp around his massive shaft, and together they began to move in their own perfect dance.

Sophie, lying on the water as her legs kept hold around his waist, arched her back. This allowed Todd to move faster and harder, thrusting deep into her core, burying his cock fully within her hungrily craving depths. Sophie's tits bobbed on the water as if they too were dancing. They floated, calling out to him.

His passion ascended to new levels as her contractions caressed his cock like a blowjob. The molten friction felt incredible. Her wet notch, so tight it felt like a suction cup pulling on him, forcing him into animalistic motions.

He rubbed her firm bud as he thrust into her, pulled out, and then slammed forward in relentless waves. Todd couldn't help feeling that he had met the woman of his dreams: adventurous, sexual, an exhibitionist to the hilt!

"Sophie, you're fucking great. You're so tight. I've wanted to fuck you since the first moment I saw you. Oh God…you're such a turn-on. You're perfect. Oh…oh…fuck yeah!"

He could tell she was turned on by a man who talked during sex, as her body undulated against him in cadence to his words. Each time he yelled out, her body responded in a convulsive heave of release.

"Fuck me! Oh yeah. Fuck me harder!" she bellowed.

Todd could feel her cresting with each pump of his hips. He knew the time had come. His desire erupted. He pushed deeper, one thrust, then a second, then a final explosion of bliss as his release saturated her. "God yeah!" he gasped.

Sophie's body melted to his. She laid her head on his shoulder and hugged him tightly. He returned her embrace and silently, listened to their muted, ragged breathing. Whereas some people go a lifetime searching for the perfect fit, Todd believed he had found his just by stopping to help a stranded motorist on a sunny day.

Sophie looked up at Todd as he squeezed her ass lightly. "I think I spoke too soon," she said.

"About what?" he replied.

"Well, let's just say that today I've had two very powerful machines between my thighs."

Todd laughed at her inventive statement, and kissed her hungrily, once again igniting their passion.

CHAPTER 10

I had been dating a young man for a brief period of time, when out of the blue he told me we needed to spice up our sex life. Now, being the erotic individual that I am, I set out one morning to surprise him with some new game, toy, or sexual endeavor.

To my amazement, my lover surprised me first. He aided me in reliving my college days, when it was my awestruck fantasy to have more than one partner at the same time. My story will unfold before you; however, I want you never to underestimate your man or woman…if they are in tune with your sexuality, they can bring you joys untold.

Coupling

I closed the door behind me and hollered, "I'm home," as I slipped off my coat and hung it on the hall tree. The silence in the house bewildered me, for I had assumed that Derrick was home. Receiving no reply, I marched upstairs and began to strip off my clothing, layer by layer—yearning for a hot bath and the imminent arrival of my handsome stud. I released a sigh of exhilaration as my satin bra dropped to the floor and I shimmied out of my panties.

Entering the bathroom, I bent over to adjust the spa jets and turn on the bath water. Abruptly, Derrick's delightfully familiar hands grabbed me about the waist and pulled my smooth naked body to him. As my bare buttocks came into contact with his fully engorged manhood, he rumbled throatily, "I know you love surprises, so I'm giving you someone special."

"Someone?" I asked with curiosity.

My passion ascended as my thoughts traveled in fond reminiscence to one ménage `a trois I had toyed with in college. I barely had enough time to draw up the memory, when the bathroom door squeaked, and from behind, there appeared an exquisitely formed Valkyrie. Her blonde hair enshrouded her; the tousled shoulder-length curls parted just enough to reveal her tantalizing beauty. Her toned body glistened in the moist heat of the tub, and the heady scent of her natural perfume wafted through the steam.

Derrick's swollen trunk pulsed heavy and hard against my tight ass, begging entry with each unconscious beat. I shivered when he swept my hair up into a knot and whispered hungrily into my ear, "This is Sherry."

Eager, yet apprehensive, I didn't move. Derrick began nibbling on my throat and the luscious creature before me approached.

Admiring Sherry's exquisite form, I licked my lips. "Sherry...hmm...that's my favorite liqueur. A little tart, meant to be savored."

Desire ignited through my being as Sherry knelt down on the floor before me, and peered up into my eyes without saying a word. While I was relishing the feeling of Sherry breathing heatedly onto my most sensitive flesh, Derrick pushed me forward slightly, grabbed my ass in his hands, and began to massage it. Every nerve ending in my body became electrified as Sherry's tongue flicked friskily against my knee then slowly made its ascent to the moist welcoming folds between my quivering thighs.

Reveling in sweet torment, I grasped the back of Sherry's hair and pulled her from her knees to a standing position, where she began playfully pinching my nipples. Without letting go of the perfectly hardened buds, she kissed me feverishly on the mouth. Our tongues met in a frenzied pace, synchronized to Derrick's every squeeze. "Oh, what pleasures," I thought as a moan escaped my lips. I reached around Sherry and softly grazed my hands over her ass.

I knew that I could climax quickly enjoying the stimulation of both sexes; however, I wanted to savor the pleasures I imagined Sherry would bring me. Hastily, I pulled away from Derrick and told Sherry to lie down on the floor. I gazed hungrily as she obeyed my command. I was overwhelmed with desire. I wanted to please her as much as I needed her to satisfy me. Kneeling down between Sherry's inviting, openly spread thighs, I allowed the first flick of my tongue to tease her feminine beauty. I smiled inwardly as she closed her eyes, momentarily lost in what could only be ecstasy. At that moment, I wanted nothing more than to devour her from head to toe.

Enthralled by this kinky endeavor, I was somewhat startled to hear Derrick above me. I wanted him to experience this grand adventure with me, so I removed my tongue from Sherry's delicacy, gestured vaguely and whispered, "Derrick, the bag at the bottom of the stairs, get it and join us." I knew that Derrick would obey my request, so I delved back into Sherry's deliciously tempting treat.

It didn't take long for Sherry to swap positions with me and initiate pleasures on my flesh. She first began by sucking my tight nipples, then skimming her hands over the tender silkiness of my skin she rested her fingers in-between the softly parted folds of my womanhood. Sherry's questing fingers teased the depths of my slick flesh while her other hand played skillfully with my breasts.

I was lost in overwhelming bliss. My back arched off the floor as Sherry worked her way down my body, replacing her dexterous fingers with her limber tongue. Involuntarily, I clasped Sherry's head tightly against my aching need. My buttocks tightened with each gentle stroke of her tongue, moving me closer with every lick to the pinnacle of climax.

In a haze of passion, I glanced up and saw Derrick standing naked, intently watching us. Uninhibited, he reached down, clutched his shaft and moved his hand methodically, as his dick jutted outward, hard and erect. Absorbing Derrick's stroking dance, I gasped, "Take out the silver box."

Derrick tore into the pink paper bag he had retrieved from downstairs, momentarily letting go of his swollen manhood. He took out a silvery package, opened it and laid it on the floor. An array of sensual delights decorated its interior. "Which one?" he asked eagerly.

"Your choice," I moaned through clenched teeth.

I didn't see which item he chose, but as he eased his way over behind Sherry, the familiar humming of the blue dolphin vibrator with anal attachment began. Watching his facial expressions, I could tell how turned-on he had become. His hand-motions looked blurred from my position and as he thrust himself within his own grip, I felt my ardor burgeoning to climax.

Masturbation always turned me on, and watching Derrick stroke his cock as Sherry's tongue licked my clit brought me quickly to the brink. My lungs expanded until I could no longer hold back and my scream of delight filled the room. "Yes! Fuck, yes! I'm coming!"

When my eyes finally fluttered open again, I saw Sherry's hips pumping and pushing back to meet every one of Derrick's hand thrusts. Her body shook violently, and I could tell by her facial expressions that she was climaxing. Within seconds Derrick exploded, his distended cock erupting, spurting his seed across Sherry's smooth backside.

"Too bad everyone's finished," I said with a pout.

To my delight, when Derrick moved from behind Sherry, his still fully-erect member came into view. I licked my lips and said, "Hey, stud, I know where you can stick that." Then turning to Sherry, I beckoned, "Come here and sit that pretty pussy on my face."

Neither one hesitated to move into their requested positions to satisfy *my* demands. Sherry straddled my face, positioning herself to face Derrick, who had already taken sanctuary between my thighs. As he eased my legs to either side of his waist, he inched forward, dipping between the luscious lips of my tempting beauty.

I began to nibble carefully on Sherry's ripe bud, while Derrick teased the emptiness of my shaded recesses. Within moments Derrick came to rest fully within my clenching core, moving to meet my rising desire. As Sherry aggressively undulated on my dexterous tongue, I began humming in conjunction with her every movement, bringing her quickly to a heightened frenzy, forcing a fast and furious release.

When she was through riding the waves of her orgasm, Sherry lifted herself off my face and turned to taste my hard-tipped breasts. She pulled one nipple deep within her mouth and rolled the other between her fingers, at the same time watching Derrick thrust his steely hardness into my pussy over and over again.

I was in heaven, experiencing a feeling that bordered on frantic. With my face free of Sherry's desire, my lungs unearthed my final, primal release.

The room filled with the scent of combined pleasures and the sound of gasping breaths and heated moans. Having all been thoroughly satisfied, we collapsed onto the floor in a tangle of spent flesh. Then, as if in a game of Clue, looking from one to the other, each of us wondered how the evening would proceed. Who would do what next to whom, with what tool, and in what room?

CHAPTER 11

One summer I found myself drifting between my sexual need for a man and my want of a woman. I came to the conclusion that life is too short not to experience the fullness and bountiful array of sensual pleasures available to one who is willing to experiment.

My travels led me to the blue door of a brazenly captivating woman. In her arms I found sweet love and the passionate fulfillment I longed for. With her, I experienced tantalizing pleasures with both women and men. Our story unfolds...

Tag Team

The town thermometer read a sweltering ninety degrees, with humidity so damn high that tank tops adhered to bodies like second skins. After walking only a couple of blocks, I desperately pulled the clinging material from my sweat-soaked cleavage and blew a cool breath of air across my bare breasts. A dashing, dark-haired stranger locked eyes with me and lifted his glass to toast my innovation in air-conditioning. A brilliant smile lit up his face and prompted me to smile in return. He sat beneath a blue canopy at Tony's Restaurant, and when he waved me over to his table, I lifted my hand in acknowledgment, stepped off the curb, and boldly ventured across the street.

I was excited to have an admirer pursuing me, for in this town the pickings were slim and women far outnumbered men. I quickened my stride as a welcomed wonder thrummed through me and I envisioned the amazing new escapade that might await me.

"Hello," the man said in a deep, powerful rumble, standing as I approached the table.

My heart skipped a beat as I briefly fantasized what his voice would sound like rough with passion. "Hello to you," I replied lightheartedly. Then, saying nothing more, I sat down and gazed at his long, slim fingers, picturing them caressing my ass as he lay naked and sweaty beneath me.

When I waved my hand in the air, it didn't take long for the waiter to materialize. In this town it paid to be a regular at every establishment, and since the waiter knew me, he delivered two shot glasses of tequila and two bottles of Pacifico for our drinking pleasure before even asking if we wanted something to eat.

The man eyed the shot glasses with a raised brow. I reached out, took his hands and cradled them in my own. Having noticed that his warm, well-manicured hands bore no ring marks or tan lines, I assumed he was fair game for my pleasures. I raised his hand to my mouth and tentatively licked the web of skin between his forefinger and thumb. I felt his body shudder and heard his breath catch in a strangled gasp.

Encouraged by his reaction, I nibbled gently, thoroughly wetting a small area on his hand with my flexible tongue. Then I coated it with a deft sprinkle from the saltshaker, drew his hand to my mouth, and licked off the salt.

A slyly devilish grin appeared on my face when the stranger grazed his teeth across his bottom lip. I could see that my advances aroused him. I dropped his hand, reached for my shot of tequila, tossed back my head, and gulped it down. Then I lifted a lemon wedge to my mouth. My sharp white teeth bit vigorously into the yellow flesh of the lemon, and the sour bite it delivered to my tongue electrified my taste buds.

The man searched my eyes, obviously trying to guess my agenda. From the smoldering look in his gaze, I knew he craved my body. I continued to tease him unmercifully, loving every minute, sucking the lemon while hoping a lurid sexual fantasy was playing out in his mind. I assumed that he was imagining me tasting the sleek tip of his manhood, running my tongue down to the base of his shaft, then racing back up again, enclosing him fully in my mouth, leaving him desperately craving more.

I was torturing myself with these thoughts, so I discarded the lemon, raised the Pacifico to my lips and met his lusty stare in recognition of our mutual desire. The idea of feasting on his thick, fleshy root had aroused me, and a feverish craving coursed over me like porn stars in a Eucalyptus shower. My clit tingled and my feminine path clenched as I envisioned him thrusting his shaft deep inside me, delighting me, bringing me to the pinnacle of total ecstasy.

When the man withdrew his money clip and waved the waiter over with a folded bill, I put out my hand and asked to see his driver's license. He handed it to me without question, as if to reassure me he was safe. I quickly scanned the picture and information. His name was Brett. He lived in Long Beach, California. He weighed 205 pounds. He stood six foot two. And he would be forty-two in June.

"Since you're from out of town, I'd be delighted if you'd let me show you the finest this town has to offer," I said, handing him back his identification. I decided not to disclose my own name. "Besides, my house is just a few blocks away, and the city view is incredible."

"Your plan sounds divinely inspired," he replied, standing up and extending his hand.

Gladly, I accepted the warmth of his touch, and together we left the restaurant. When we rounded the corner of Rally Street, I pointed to a bright blue door. "There's home," I chirped, walking across the street. Like a puppy, Brett followed me, obviously intrigued.

I entered the bungalow and closed the door, decisively securing Brett's fate with a turn of the lock. The silence between us broke quickly when a throaty, sex-filled voice drifted down the stairs. "Sunny? Is that you?"

"Why, of course it is," I replied, loving the pet name she had given me.

"Did you get the wine?"

"No. But I brought something even better. Why don't you come take a peek?"

My eyes never left Brett's. His widened in mystification at the unfolding of events and when his stare moved cautiously towards the banister, I smirked knowingly. My fiery redheaded girlfriend strode towards the landing. Brett's awestruck ogle homed in on the rose tattoo that wound its way up her inner thigh. Again he bit his bottom lip as he had done at the restaurant and exhaled deeply as he took in her lovely, naked form.

I watched as my lover floated lightly down the stairs, extending her right hand to Brett. "Sorry if I startled you."

Brett took her hand, raised it to his lips, then turned it over and kissed the sensitive skin of her palm. "God, I'm lucky," he choked.

"How do you like my surprise, Rose?" I asked, leaning in to softly kiss her supple lower lip.

"Aren't we sharing him?" Rose inquired after licking her lip, savoring the hint of lemon my kiss had left.

My eyes dropped below Brett's belt, the beat of his heart obviously working overtime as the pulsing under his pants danced on its own. "Oh, yeah. There's more than enough to go around," I purred, motioning for Rose to take hold of one of Brett's hands while I took the other. Together we led him up the stairs and into the bedroom.

Rose knelt on the bed in front of us. Cast adrift in lust, I watched Rose grab hold of Brett's shirt, ripping through the fine silk, and dragging his willing body onto the bed. As she lay on her back, Brett delved immediately into her delicate bouquet, inhaling her personal scent, and then quickly turned her over on top of him. Wantonly she embraced his shoulders with her thighs and placed her sodden pussy onto his eagerly awaiting tongue, facing me.

Meanwhile, I angled myself to inspect Brett's bared, chiseled chest. Unable to control my desire, I disrobed, straddled his legs and reached down to unleash his swollen cock from its bondage of clothing. Once it emerged, I rose onto my knees and positioned the silken head of his pulsating, vein-laden prick against the drenched heat of my quivering pussy.

I gyrated up and down atop Brett. His skilled cock penetrated me, diving frenetically into and out of my core. My motions became spasmodic as my loins squeezed and released him. Brett reached down and grabbed hold of my ass: kneading my tender flesh, pulling my body close to his, forcing me to pump and grind with a vengeance. The more I moved, the closer I came to release; my tightly coiled walls intimately clung to every inch of his throbbing rod in sweet bliss.

Brett must have read my body's desires, for he slapped my ass sharply with one hand as my excitement mounted. I opened my eyes and found myself peering into Rose's face, longingly, as she moved atop Brett's tongue. I knew well Rose's intimate expressions and realized instantly that my lover's peak was imminent. I watched as she rode Brett's face and his fingers explored her tight recesses.

I hungered to share my climax with Rose, so I leaned in to steal a warm kiss of our devotion. Rose's mouth opened, granting my tongue access. Tenderly searching, our tongues twined in a kiss, so gentle, yet delivered with such rapture that it unfurled our tightly coiled orgasms. I felt my warmth saturate Brett's cock, and he came with a violent eruption of his sex. Rose's cries became incoherent with each wave of her release.

As my breathing slowed, I lifted myself off Brett's depleted flesh and collapsed exhausted on the bed to recover feeling in my thighs. Rose moved in next to me and laid her head lovingly on my stomach. Brett did not move. The three of us lay completely spent. Bathed with the merest hint of musk, our exquisitely satisfied forms melded as one.

This playful afternoon reminded me that it's okay to stray from your shopping list, and pick up the goodies you really want.

CHAPTER 12

It must be said that although I prefer to spend my time in the tropics wearing little to nothing, every once in awhile the mountaincaps' siren song calls out to me. The allure of a roaring fire, snow bunnies in tight fitting leggings, and men without morals sometimes tempts me to jump into my 4X4 and take off for snow covered peaks.

For this trip I procured the company of Kristal and Tiffany, my two best friends in the world. Within minutes they packed and our threesome was off to Whistletop Ski Lodge. As my friends coursed down the slopes of Black Diamond Trails, I preferred to pursue a more leisurely pastime: hunting down the best looking gentleman on the mountain. Sometimes it takes a blizzard of icy snow to heat up a lustful afternoon.

Snowbound

Anticipation filled me. I felt a surge of electricity thrum through my veins as I approached the illuminated front door of the ski chalet. I chose this lodge for many reasons. Currently the lounge and circular fire pit beckoned me. I craved the tempting sweet cream of a Bailey's and coffee and the warmth of the roaring fire to caress my backside.

I wore my tight fitted black and cobalt blue suede pants and a stark white eyelet and lace, almost Victorian bustier under my jacket. I wanted to give the idea that I was too naughty to put on a shirt. I sauntered across the floor and took a seat on the couch in front of the fire pit. It didn't take long for the waiter to appear.

"What can I get you?" he inquired helpfully.

"Let me see," I replied scanning the lounge. Playfully I stated, "I'll take the gentleman in the hunter green sweater at the bar. Oh yeah, can you bring me a Bailey's and coffee on your way back?"

The waiter grinned, and then disappeared. When he returned he carefully set my coffee down on a coaster and then handed me a napkin. "Sean's reply is on this," he said as I took the napkin from him.

I hesitated to look at the napkin. Instead I raised a brow in Sean's direction and caught him staring back. Our eyes met. Chemistry!

He seemed to sit a bit straighter in his chair as I itemized his attributes from a distance. His bright pearly whites shone against the bronze color of his flesh. His burnt auburn hair curled against the nape of his neck and the edge of his form fitting sweater. His locks emphasized his eyes, the deep sea-green color of the ocean. He raised a brow to me and winked as my scrutiny continued down his physique. His muscular arms flexed within the skin tight binding of his sweater. To make the moment more memorable, I lifted my coffee to my lips, drew in a taste and then gestured for him to stand and turn around so that I could continue my inspection.

Instead of standing and turning around, he stood, pushed in his stool, took his drink in hand and made his way to the couch where I lounged.

"Don't you care what's on the napkin?" he asked his voice husky and deep.

"Not as much as I care what's in the package," I bantered back eyeballing the inseam of his pants. I drew in another sip of my drink slowly, savoring the delicate sweetness of the cream, and then purposefully traced the outline of my lips with my tongue. "I bet mine is sweeter than yours," I dared.

"Mind if I sit down, before I'm not functionally able to?"

I motioned for him to take a seat next to me. He was confident, I like that. He appeared to be a man who was not afraid to succumb to a woman's desires. I wanted to feel him surrender to passion, under the skilled mastery of my body. If I toyed long enough with the appetizer I would be assured the nine course banquet with dessert tray.

Once again Sean eyed the napkin. Reaching down, I lifted my coffee to the side and drew the napkin into my lap where I unfolded it. Written in black ink was, "I give a great massage. My office keys are on the bar waiting for your answer."

"You go girl," I thought to myself gazing back at the stud next to me. It had been some time since I had tempted the pleasures of the flesh with such a fine specimen. If he was as talented in other areas as he was in his ability to move me with words then I was in for a tongue tied evening. I actually found myself flustered. He had caught me off guard with his forthright advances and I needed to sit in silence for a moment.

Once again he spoke, "Are you feeling tight anywhere?" he inquired. Then with a twinkle in his eye and a quick wink he slipped me a business card: Sean O'Malley—Licensed Massage Therapist—Whistletop Ski Lodge.

"Aha," I replied. "You bad little boy you. I must admit that you play a good game."

"Who's playing?" he asked before saying in a taunting manner, "Little Bo Peep in her suede pants appears to have had a run in with the Big Bad Wolf and skinned him. I was just hoping to get her lined up and in perfect formation so that any others who might want to lead her astray would not. In my care, she'll be well tended to."

"Nursery rhymes, limericks and business cards. Do you score more often with the college students who can only understand simple fables and tall tales or are you equally successful in the big leagues with those of us who want it all?"

"My seven o'clock canceled her appointment. Are you interested in being pampered from head to toe?"

"Always," I replied.

"I'll send the waiter over with a key to the ladies' lounge area. You can undress there."

Realizing that he must keep up the appearance of professionalism in the work place I let him go. I knew, as all women do, that this man wanted more than just to give me a massage. I looked forward to encouraging him. I welcomed the company and anxiously watched for the return of the waiter.

I felt giddy and my stomach fluttered in excitement. My girlfriends were still out skiing and here I was about to attack the finest looking man on the mountain. Something had drawn me into the lounge earlier than normal, and oh yeah, was I thankful. My loins grew moist as I imagined him gliding his large masculine hands across my bare flesh. I sensed that he would be a tenacious, yet patient lover; a man who would offset his own pleasure to satisfy the woman in his arms.

I withdrew some cash in order to pay my tab. The waiter appeared, a broad smile reflecting from his face. "Here are the keys to the ladies' lounge. The door is to the left of the bar." He flashed me a little wink and then continued, "Have a wonderful evening. Please come visit us again soon."

"Always a pleasure," I replied.

I rose. My mind raced as my subconscious yelled, "Get going girl. You deserve to have some fun!" I reached down and lifted my mug, carefully taking it with me toward the lounge door and the muscular masseur who waited to caress my silky, bronzed, flesh and to transport me to another realm under the magical touch of his skillful hands.

The key fit snugly into the lock and the door opened with ease. The ladies' lounge was a beautifully ornate room where you disrobed and prepared for your massage or spa treatment. Sean had placed a plush cranberry red robe and hair tie on the sofa and there was light music playing in the background.

I undressed, careful to hang my belongings up as they were shed. Being the only person in the room, I admired my nakedness in the full length mirror. I stared at my own lithe figure and smiled. I had treated myself to a full body wax in preparation for my mountain escape. My body was smooth and bare except for a perfectly shaped star which rested at the crest of my pubic bone. My femininity blossomed, displayed as eye candy ready to be satisfied and savored.

I twisted my long locks up into a knot and secured it with the red hair tie. I slipped into the luxuriant cranberry robe and loosely tied a make shift knot to keep it on. I took a seat on the lounge chair and sipped my drink.

"Little Bo Peep? Are you ready?" Sean's strong voice summoned through the door.

"Yeah," I replied.

I opened the door and found Sean standing in the hall dressed in formal whites and a smile passed my lips. "Where are you taking me?" I inquired laughingly.

"To my parlor, beautiful."

Excited, I eagerly followed him through a set of doors into the most breathtaking room I'd ever entered. Cathedral ceilings, wispy gossamer curtains, tall medieval looking candelabras with chunk candles already lit and a massage table covered in beautiful cream silken sheets. He started to turn around to allow me to get under the sheets unnoticed, but this is me! I demand an audience! "Do my looks offend you, Sean?" I hastily inquired.

Just as he turned around, but before he had a chance to answer I dropped my robe. I stood naked and waiting. His eyes roved my body, and stopped, briefly entranced at the star above my personal heaven. I watched him watch me. I surveyed his pants as they shifted from his apparent growing arousal; he liked what he saw and couldn't deny it.

"Lie down on your back," he instructed. "I assure you that once I've finished your massage your body will be dripping with pleasure."

Slowly, Sean pulled the sheet back.

There was no need to cover what I desired Sean to see, so as I eased my body onto the warm sheets, I instructed him to leave my body uncovered.

Haunting notes of smoky jazz music floated down from the speakers high above. Sean dimmed the lights and the illuminating glow of the flickering candles enhanced the room's aura of seduction.

Sean lifted my left hand up and breathed a heated deep moan into the fleshy mid section of my palm. I observed his calculated moves as his tongue wetted his full lips and softly he began kissing the tips of each of my fingers. When his lips met my thumb, he first kissed the top, and then drew the digit into his warm, wet mouth, like I had envisioned sucking on his cock. A strangled gasp caught in my throat and a chill ran through my body causing me to flinch.

"You cold?" he asked.

"No," I replied. "Just horny."

"Well, I'll have to see what I can do to help you with that."

He laid my hand back down upon the massage table and reached back, retrieving a bottle which lay next to my hip.

With every stroke of his fingers, heated sensations traveled over my silky skin. Tenderly he applied a warming lotion with the merest hint of sweet vanilla to my palm.

Dexterously his fingers traced patterns over my sensitive flesh, taking turns massaging each individual finger. The friction his hands created ignited my every nerve ending. Once he finished with my hand, his dutiful attention masterfully began its quest up my arm.

I had not felt such pampering in a long time, so when Sean's massage paused momentarily at my right shoulder and he leaned down to kiss the tender flesh between my breasts I actually shuddered.

"You're just too mesmerizing. Your skin is like the softest of down, and you smell delectable. I just couldn't help myself, I had to stop and taste *your* bounty," he stated matter a fact.

"Smooth talker," I replied just above a whisper. "Twelve inches lower and I'll expect more than just a kiss." I watched as Sean's face lit up and his grin sparkled.

Seamlessly he shifted his position from my side to the top end of the massage table. Sean's fingers began rubbing the back of my neck and then entwined, frolicking within my long chestnut tresses. I had to bite my lip to stop from moaning. Effortlessly he slid his hands under my neck and began to rub my upper back and shoulders. My body became putty under the assault of his strong touch.

I could feel my nipples peak as Sean's accomplished hands maneuvered to massage my left arm. With the same focus he had exhibited with my right arm, he tended to every inch of my left. The sweet vanilla oil heightened my senses and I closed my eyes momentarily, lost in exquisite euphoria. Just as I began to visualize him sliding his dick into my pussy, I felt his gentle full lips close tenderly around my hardened nipple.

My eyes fluttered open. I bit my lower lip as Sean's flexible tongue traced circular patterns around my distended buds. His mouth was warm, his tongue soft and wet, and his desire apparent. Wanting to assuage the ache of passion thrumming between my legs, I longed to force his head down, between my thighs, to my bared sex. My mindless wandering lasted only a minute. Sean withdrew his lips from my nipple and began massaging the upper slopes of my breasts. His dexterous hands moved down my ribcage then melded against my hip bones. At this juncture I thought that he would take me. I was wrong.

His talent at temptation was like no other. His sturdy hands began working down my inner thighs, his thumbs curving inward, barely grazing the delicate flesh against the outwardly budding petal of my nether lips. With the tips of his thumbs he forced a shiver to run through my body and with a devilish grin Sean moved his hands down the length of my legs in a long sweeping massage. I was on the brink. His touch, his kiss, his warm breath had left me yearning for the feel of his cock thrusting deep within me. I wanted him. I wanted to grab hold of his ass as he moved with me and dig my nails into his hips.

Instinctively my hands took hold of his. I had to stop him. "Sean. I want you now!" I demanded.

"As you wish," he replied letting go of my legs and pushing my thighs apart. "But first things first," he said as he reached up with his left hand and began softly teasing my clit with his broad thumb. He buried his face in my delicate flesh and with the first flick of his tongue against the inner lips of my feminine desire I began to squirm. His gentle teasing manner suddenly turned vigorous, forcing me to the edge. The tension in my body was building to an unbearable point.

As if he could sense what I craved, Sean moved his right hand between my thighs and inserted two long fingers inside my velvety sheath. His thumb, fingers, and tongue moved in unison. With every tiny motion his thumb made, his fingers quested deep within me and his tongue flicked and suckled. I reached up and grabbed Sean's head locking my fingers in his auburn hair. I pulled him in closer as my back arched and the unbearable tightness coiling in my loins unleashed. "Oh, God!" I called out as my body relaxed and my arms fell to the table.

Completely sated, I sighed as Sean removed his fingers from my slick glide and tenderly kissed my oversensitive, throbbing hood. "Your time isn't up yet, young lady. Turn over."

I obeyed his command and turned over onto my stomach. My body tingled, vibrantly electrified, alive with the remnants of his fiery touch and I was lost in blissful abandon.

"Lift your hips up," Sean instructed.

"Why?" I inquired.

"Are you questioning me? I mean, are you trying to tell me that you really *don't* want the full body massage?"

With a statement like that, I quickly raised my hips as Sean slipped a soft pillow under them. I knew what he was preparing for, deep penetration. Any woman who had been with a creative, well hung man knew the tricks of the trade. The pillow added angle, allowing him to impel deeper and with more finesse. I was ready for anything at this point. His hands were magical and my body had relaxed under his touch. I began thinking about what he might have in store for my further pleasure.

I felt dribbles of warm oil trickle over my upper thighs. Sean's hands slid seamlessly up and down my legs. He caressed my inner thighs, my claves, and then worked his way back up to the curve of my ass. My body was his altar and I silently moaned in blissful delight. Sensuously, he kissed both cheeks of my shapely ass and then scorched a trail from my buttocks to the nape of my neck where he kissed me feverishly. "God you're hot," he intoned huskily.

I turned my head to look at him. He stood next to me and I watched as he began to unbutton his shirt. One by one the buttons parted, revealing his sleek, muscular, sun kissed chest. I desired to reach out and touch him. I could feel myself growing even moister with excitement. My loins ached. I wanted to feel him deep within me.

It was as if he could read my unspoken thoughts. Like a Chip n' Dale dancer, he moved his shoulders and discarded his shirt. Slowly he pulled the drawstring to his trousers and they fell to the floor around his ankles. My gaze traced upwards from the floor and lay transfixed upon his extended girth. His cock hung semi-erect, flexing involuntarily. I couldn't take my eyes off him. I wanted to take his dick within the tempting warm walls of my succulent mouth and tease the tip of his cock with my tongue. I desired to touch myself and rub my clit as I drew him completely down the back of my throat.

Sean moved closer to me. My body shivered as I watched his every movement. In three steps his hardened shaft was in my face. I reached out and took hold of his ass, drawing him in to the side of the table. Teasingly I flicked my tongue against the tip of his dick. He pressed himself into me and without haste; I drew him fully within my mouth. I felt him grow with every movement I made. Sliding my tongue and my mouth in unison around him forced a muffled moan to caress his cock.

"Oh yeah," Sean gasped with a thrust of his pelvis.

I sucked his distended length harder and faster. With each movement, I squeezed his ass with my hand, moving my fingers ever closer to the taut recess of his anus. Slowly I began circling the outer puckered flesh with my oil slicked fingertips. The head of Sean's cock pulsed in my mouth and as his movements quickened, I slowly introduced my index finger with tiny increments, into the sensitive, tight entrance of his chiseled body.

"Do you want me to come?" Sean heaved with a raspy gasp.

Unwilling to remove my mouth from the temptation against my palate, I drove my finger deeper into him and hastened my movements against his slick pecker. Sean's movements became instinctive. He reached out and gripped my hair with his hands as he desperately pumped his cock against my tonsils and clenched his ass against my questing finger.

"Ohhhhh fuck yeah," he groaned as he erupted deep within my throat with spurts of pulsing ecstasy.

Throughout the last spasms of his release I milked the remnants of his desire, tenderly bathing him with my tongue.

Carefully, Sean unfurled my locks and braced himself against the table while he regained his composure.

Slowly I withdrew my finger from its intimate invasion and grazed my fingertips against his bared flesh as I returned to my prone position on the table.

Sean reached out for what I had assumed was more massaging oil, yet to my surprise he retrieved a wet towel from the warming heater and began to bathe my hands. My heightened state of sexual arousal turned frenzied when Sean's attention shifted from my hands; predatorily, he moved behind me, hoisting himself up onto the table, straddling my naked form.

My lust filled haze mounted and as Sean's fingers roamed relentlessly down the streamlined crack of my ass and slid easily into the wanting cradle of my hunger. My body writhed; twisting and turning beneath him. There was no need to fight the unquenchable desire that was now verging on desperate lust. With every stroke his fingers made deep within my liquid glide, I squeezed my muscles around him. My penchant for recklessness forced me to beg, "Oh Sean, I need more. Now!"

Sean's fingers continued their odyssey within my feminine

folds and I began to anticipate his massive girth tempting the depths of my being in an ancient, rhythmic, primal groove. Drawn from my thoughts within minutes, I felt the silken tip of Sean's dick begging entrance to the soft, shaded recesses of my desire. A new found awareness rippled through me. My body acted on its own accord as I lifted my ass, revealing to Sean his cock's very own porthole to heaven.

I bit down on my bottom lip as the head of his turgid shaft eased into me. I breathed out a somewhat garbled sigh as my body succumbed to the stiff up-thrust of Sean's dick. I was spellbound as the master masseur atop me preformed a cadenced dance that both excited and stimulated me. My body moved with his and with every spar and parry that we exchanged, the whirlwind of pleasure that I was experiencing grew stronger.

We were no longer two people—we had become one animalistic pair, bewitched by the flesh. Every movement... every stroke of his fingers...every muscular clench of my pussy against his steely hardness pressed me towards climax. My clit pulsed in desperate need as the head of his cock swelled and pranced within me. I could no longer hold back my release.

"Oh fuck, Sean. Grab my hips."

Sean passionately took hold of my hips, pulling my ass to him, fully embedding his cock deep within me.

"Come with me," he instructed.

Barely had the words escaped his lips as I cried out, "Fuck me, fuck me, oh baby don't stop. I'm coming!"

Washed over in a luster of sweat Sean collapsed on top of me and together we lay in sweet oblivion until our breathing returned to normal. Once we had recovered from our cataclysmic starburst of sexual exploits, Sean dressed and handed me my cranberry robe. Without saying a word led me down the hallway toward yet another door. Here he paused, lifted my chin up to face him and kissed me with a deep and frenzied need on the mouth.

"Ready to see what's behind door number two?" he asked.

"Ready, willing, and most definitely able," I replied with a smile. Reaching down I slipped my hands down his trousers and took his cock into my hands.

Coquettishly I peered up and said, "The question is Mr. Masseur, are you ready to show me?"

CHAPTER 13

Over the years I have received numerous letters of adoration. I am not modest by any means, so when I put pen to paper, I am inviting you to experience my stories through my eyes or through the eyes of those who have been privy to my sexual escapades. The following story I received in a care package which contained a Dictaphone and a single tape cassette.

Demarco had obviously not been afraid of the experience we shared, only of reliving it alone. In the first few minutes of the tape he reassured me that my seeing our sublime liaison through his eyes would not only exceed his grandest expectation of fulfillment but also enliven my senses.

This is for you, Demarco, the tale of our dazzling threesome, played out as you saw us that evening.

Virtue

Boredom overtook me, as a room-service dinner failed to quench my need for illicit entertainment. I was in town for only a few days, so I meandered to the elevator and went straight for the bar I had seen down the street upon my arrival in town this morning. My stride quickened as I approached the bar entrance. Once I pushed through the doors I took a seat in front of the bartender and outwardly began scanning the room for potential thrills. My sights fell upon a couple seated at the far end of the bar.

"That's incredible," I breathed, marveling at the display of affection occurring on the barstools near the jukebox. A couples kiss, delivered with such overwhelming seduction that it seized my gaze and held me transfixed.

I watched, spellbound, as their lips parted and their tongues began to explore, thoroughly impressed by their erotic exhibitionism. My eyes ventured, beyond their exploits to examine the woman's sensual body. My heart skipped a beat. Her beauty, barely covered by a flimsy dress, captivated me. The fullness of her lips beckoned as the man's white teeth raked softly against her bottom lip, finding refuge in her brazen sexuality. I couldn't help but bite down on my own lip, wishing that I too had some exotic woman to devour at that very moment.

The man was tall and his wavy chestnut hair magnified his large deep-green eyes. He caressed the woman's neck with a noticeably soft touch as he kissed her mouth slowly and longingly.

Although the couple seemed oblivious to their surroundings, I sensed that they were actually aroused by the attention of the audience around them. I felt tortured. I squirmed in my seat as my manhood stirred to life; the carnal desire forcing a fire to burn deep within me.

The woman began slowly rubbing her long fingers through her partner's hair. Then she tugged his head back gently and applied her teeth to his neck. Not a soul in the bar was blind to their hunger, yet not a soul approached. No one stepped forward to interrupt them or to join in their fun.

In the past, my apprehension surrounding possible rejection had stopped me from approaching other swingers, even in a bar such as this; one known for kinky play and partner sharing. Yet this time was different. My desire for the woman's luscious form propelled me to action.

Preparing to proposition the couple, I scooted back my barstool, but stopped when I suddenly felt a wisp of soft hair against my cheek. I froze. I didn't dare turn around. I thought my imagination had caught up to me, until someones delicate fingers, sinuously intertwined with my hair and carefully pulled my head back, demanding my attention.

Turning cautiously, I came face to face with the tantalizing couple. No coherent thoughts stirred in my mind; instead I stared in amazement at the pair. When my eyes met the man's, he extended one of his bronzed, well-weathered hands towards me. "The name's Slade. And the gorgeous creature massaging your scalp is Ms. Chastity."

Chuckling, I shook Slade's hand. Chastity leaned forward and lustily whispered into my ear, "I hope your key can open my box."

A devilish grin passed my lips. She had delivered the invitation. Reaching up, I withdrew her hand from my hair, raised it to my lips, and mischievously nibbled the tips of her fingers before placing an affectionate kiss on the palm of her hand. Her low, gentle murmur indicated that she craved more. I guided her hand into the pocket of my sport coat. Her hand emerged with a set of hotel keys dangling from her delicate, French manicured fingertips.

Not a word passed between us. I motioned towards the door, acknowledging that I had accepted their compelling, unspoken invitation. After leaving some money on the bar to cover my tab, I led us toward the beckoning unknown.

The cool night air streaked across my face. My blood raced through my veins and my heart beat like thunder in my chest, awakening my senses. My cock swelled, pushing against my zipper with restrained ferocity. My entire being thrummed with excitement.

I was grateful that the hotel I had reserved was on the same block as the bar. Within minutes we entered the hotel lobby. I pressed the arrow on the wall and envisioned the night to come and the sexual play in store for me. Seconds later the elevator doors parted, allowing our trio entrance to the small, well-insulated space. My breathing became erratic. The wait seemed unbearable. Yet, as the doors secured and the outside world ceased to exist, calm swept the elevator. A new realm of pleasure was about to open for me. "Let the games begin," I breathed.

Reaching out with longing and lustful intent, I pushed Chastity against the surface of Slade's muscular chest, and inched my way towards her. As my body meshed with hers, my throbbing dick pulsed against the light, silky fabric of her dress, and the heat radiating from her body roused me to heights I had only experienced in vivid daydreams. I didn't have a chance to take further playful or seductive action upon my captive duo before the elevator stopped and the doors parted.

My room-key found sanction in its porthole, and I pushed forcefully on the door, gaining entrance into the room. Chastity assumed responsibility for initiating the night's pleasures, hypnotizing my entire being with her erotic presence. My eyes trailed her movements as she sauntered towards the king-size bed. I reached down and began rubbing my turgid shaft through its covering, unabashedly conscious of my audience.

I watched as Slade slipped the tiny spaghetti straps from Chastity's shoulders, invitingly displaying the perfection of her breasts. Her rosy pink nipples, hardened with passion, seemed to beg for my attention with their slightly upward tilt. Releasing my grip on my shaft, I stalked like a feral predator closer to the duo.

I was mesmerized by Chastity's tantalizing beauty. Succumbing to my need, I reached out, grabbed the edge of her dress, tugged lightly, and watched as it pooled around her dainty ankles. "What a delicious morsel," I exhaled, as Chastity's glory was unveiled before me. I stared at her sleekly muscled legs and licked my lips with desperate hunger.

Captivated by the thin line of tight curls at the apex of her thighs, I sighed long and deep. Between her toned legs lay my portal to heaven. The neatly trimmed strip of brunette curls, already glistening with the dew of her passion, taunted me. Her swollen lips parted slightly, beckoning, and as I gazed on in a daze of lust, the slick dark pink of her inner lips summoned me to action.

I lowered my head as if in prayer and began kissing Chastity's lush breasts. I accosted her nipples heatedly, capturing each one within my lips, then teased it for a moment before letting it go. As Chastity moaned, my teeth grasped one nipple while my fingers searched for, and then clasped the other. Lightly, I pulled, twisted and nibbled, assuaging her demanding desire.

I felt the urgent need to free myself of my clothing. Not wanting to douse Chastity's incandescent fire, I rose cautiously, all the while continuing my attentive movements until I was able to grab Slade's arm and motion him to take over my position. Without hesitation, Slade maneuvered to savor Chastity's succulent breasts in my absence. I looked on in silent anticipation as I quickly shed my shirt, stepped out of my Dockers, then purposefully positioned myself behind Chastity's exquisitively naked form.

My hands reached out. Tracing their own route, I started at the back of Chastity's neck, then gradually let them glide down the length of her body, finally coming to rest on her mouthwatering, heart-shaped ass. I cupped, groped, squeezed and polished her smooth round cheeks with my hands.

I smiled, knowing my lavish touch brought Chastity an array of pleasure. Surrendering to my mastery she sighed, leaning into Slade's caress, her body quivering. My breath caught in my throat as my lust emerged rock hard, a driving force needing to be reckoned with.

From the first display of sexual intent at the bar, I had envisioned what a skilled lover Chastity might be. Brazenly, she aided me in finding her pulsing sex, and my fingers intertwined with hers, invading her slick, velvety channel. My excitement escalated exponentially as I watched Slade drop to his knees to worship at Chastity's bared altar in front of us.

In the hopes of stoking her flame, I slapped Chastity on the ass, forcing her to clench her body's openings. The quick pang of my spanking compelled her to widen her stance, instantly accommodating the exquisite invasion Slade perpetrated. I was overwhelmed with excitement, knowing that my fingers had prepared her tight channel for more. I eagerly rocked my swollen shaft between the cleft of her cheeks, simultaneously kneading and exploring.

When I could no longer remain a passive partner, I gave in to my animal instincts and forcefully pulled Chastity away from Slade's amorous attention. I urged her supple body to bend forward, opening her to me as my hands seized her hipbones.

Chastity's hands came to rest on the floor, sending her buttocks in the air. They demanded I fill her further with passion. I was entranced by her sweet pussy, which seemed to pulse in reaction to her inner spasms. She panted, "Ride me."

I obeyed, maneuvering my steely hardness into her depths, dipping within to taste her sweet nectar. She pushed herself back against me, forcing me to impale myself in her heated core. Unleashing my hunger, plunging deep and hot within her, I pulled her ass to meet my every thrust.

When Chastity screamed, "Fuck me! Fuck me! Oh God, you're fucking me so good!" I felt her inner muscles contracting rhythmically in spasms of delight.

Through half-open eyes, I observed Slade as he unzipped his pants, positioned himself in front of Chastity and began stroking his engorged length, performing for her while she preformed for me. His long, thick cock danced in front of Chastity's passion-contorted face, and as she sensuously rolled her tongue across the crown of his pulsing need, she drew his entire length into her mouth. I sensed Slade burgeoning on release. When Chastity's motions became more aggressive his breathing grew husky and deep and his body shuddered, forcing him to fall to his knees to recover.

With Slade finally out of the way, I demanded that Chastity stand up. I levered myself, remaining deep within her, my chest melding against her smooth back, as I raised her arms about my neck. Placing a strong arm around her slender waist, I continued my exploration of her scalding softness until I could no longer control my lustful craving. My pace became frantic and I writhed with animalistic hunger.

As if knowing that my orgasm hinged on her every nasty word, Chastity screamed out, "You dirty boy. Keep fucking me with your huge cock! You're great. Oh yeah. Fuck me. Yeah, fuck me hard. Oh baby, don't stop!"

I felt a surge of Chastity's warm, sweet juices lubricating my cock as my life force exploded. I came with such vigor that my teeth sank into my bottom lip. Without releasing her waist I held Chastity tight as I pumped the remainder of my seed deep into her.

Having all been temporarily satisfied, it didn't take long for us to collapse onto the bed in a mound of spent flesh. I was the first to speak. I looked from Slade to Chastity, then back again. I said, "Thanks for the wonderfully satisfying introduction." While still breathing raggedly I continued, "I know now that the saying is true...swingers truly do liven up an evening."

CHAPTER 14

I cannot say I tired of playing with more than one partner, but the adoration of one is a pleasure I relish.

Having the attention of a lover solely on me makes me feel like a goddess being worshiped. One eventful day, I helped my best friend in her move across town. When she stepped out to run her errands, I assumed her identity. During her absence, I let her new neighbor be my welcoming committee and oh what a housewarming gift!

The Girl Next Door

The neighbor turned his car into the drive, parked and got out. Like a love-struck schoolboy, he stood staring at me. The doors to the U-Haul were ajar, and inside were numerous boxes marked with their respective destinations: kitchen, bathroom and bedroom. I stood holding the box marked "bedroom." I knew that caught his eye. Teasingly, I pretended not to notice his fascination with me.

My hair feathered out to fall in highlighted layers— colored strands ranging from the lightest of blondes to deep mahogany. My stylist said that the spectrum of colors blended to form the perfect frame for my pixie-like features. Under my dirty, sweaty, moving-day white tank top, the darkened area of my areolas showed, clearly revealing the absence of a bra. I felt his smoldering gaze admiring my breasts. The rest of my attire consisted of buckskin Timberland boots and a daringly short, pale yellow sunflower-print skirt. Under my skirt I wore a tiny silken pair of white G-string panties.

Purposely I bent over to grab a box just as a strong wind blew, billowing my skirt up onto my back. I chuckled. I knew he was standing behind me, assuredly thinking that the gods were on his side, having just exposed my delectably firm backside for him to see. I didn't move an inch to reposition my skirt; I simply waited for gravity to take effect. When my skirt drifted back into its original place, I turned coyly and looked over in his direction.

He was eyeing me like a male animal during rutting season looking for a chance to pounce. I deliberately dropped the box I was holding. It fell onto the driveway and broke apart, sprawling its contents out all over the pavement. Panties of various colors everywhere: flaming red, shimmering black, emerald green, even some with little pale pink flowers, lay strewn all over the ground in front of him. Silk and cotton, jockeys and thongs spilled in a colorful, erotic rainbow before him.

His eyes widened with lustful and shocked arousal. I assumed he was imagining me clothed in the scandalous scraps of fabric. Saying nothing, I bent over and began to pick up the garments, never taking my eyes off his, silently demanding conversation.

He squatted next to me and started helping me pick up the scattered panties. "Sorry I startled you," he said gruffly.

"That's alright," I replied.

"My name's Bruce," he said as he extended his hand, holding a pair of fuchsia thong panties in his grasp.

I reached out, taking the panties in lieu of his hand. "Sari," I lied. Knowing that assuming my friend's name might one day get her into trouble. I silently chuckled, "What's life without a little trouble?"

When Bruce finally placed the undergarments back into the box, he rose to his feet. With a twinkle in his eye, he looked to me and said, "Since we're neighbors, want to join me for a little barbecue?"

Wondering how far I should take this masquerade and how long Sari would actually be gone, I decided not to reply.

"Well, that is, if you don't have a better offer already?" he tried again.

"Actually, I'm starving," I admitted, knowing good and well that this would be more than just a barbecue. It had been some time since I had engaged in a delightful sexual encounter and I was way overdue.

Bruce looked past me into the truck. "Why don't you let me help you finish unloading in the morning?"

"Yeah, right," I joked. "The new girl in town accepts an invite to barbeque, and her neighbor promises that he'll help her unpack in the morning."

"You must be kidding. After seeing the contents of this box, I can't wait to see the hidden treasures nestled in the rest."

"Okay. We have a deal then," I said, sure that Sari would appreciate my ingenuity in the morning.

I knew she had a dozen things on her list to do and that she would be away for at least a couple of hours more. With an anticipatory thrill, I locked the U-Haul door and retrieved my purse and travel bag from the front seat. I turned to Bruce. "Mind if I freshen up at your house? I don't have a clue where my towels are."

"My house is your house," he stated, gesturing up the sidewalk. We strolled forward in companionable silence, and he gallantly held the door open for me. "The bathroom is the first door on the left."

Flashing him a wonder-girl smile, I sauntered down the hall to the bathroom. My backside felt scorched by his heated scrutiny of my shapely ass swaying from side to side.

"Thank God for neighbors," he whispered throatily, just loud enough for me to hear.

As I turned on the water in the bathroom shower, I imagined him undressing me. I visualized his strong, sun-kissed hands pulling the clothes from my sweat-drenched skin. Stepping naked into the warm water, I envisioned him washing my back, leaving a stimulating trail of electricity in his fingers' wake. A lance of sensation burgeoned between my thighs as the water cascaded down my front. My nipples formed hard peaks in the pelting spray. My lust transformed into an elemental entity with every erotic image that flooded my mind. I knew that I had to get out of the shower before I succumbed to my own tangled longings.

I returned to the kitchen, my drenched tresses resembling the blackness of licorice vines, my body brazenly clad in men's boxers and a thin white cotton tank top. Still ensconced in my steamy fantasy, I heard him say, "I have a hot tub out back. No suits required."

"Now?" I bent over and reached into my bag to retrieve a bottle of wine I had bought to christen Sari's new home. "Where do you keep your wine glasses?" I inquired as I dangled the bottle of Merlot.

Trying to contain his apparent jubilation, but failing miserably, he grabbed some candles that were sitting on the counter and motioned for me to follow him.

"Glasses?" I prompted with an impish grin.

"Glasses. To the left of the dishwasher in the hutch. I'll get the corkscrew."

Carrying the glasses and wine, I followed him down the hall. Bruce paused momentarily at the linen closet and grabbed two towels. Towels in hand, he pushed open the back-door screen, revealing a magnificent ocean view. I stood, mesmerized by my surroundings. The sun rested on the water, lingering in Technicolor profusion as it does during the moments before twilight.

I studied Bruce as he placed the candles on the step, then lifted the hot tub cover and pulled it to the lawn. By the time he turned around, the steam rising from the water had enshrouded my naked form. I stood unabashed as he surveyed my body, following the line of my silhouette. His eyes traveled slowly, taking in the true essence of my being, from my silken breasts to my slender waistline. Then, scanning the gently rounded fullness of my hips, he paused; savoring the sight of the clean shaven V nestled between my chiseled thighs. I stepped into the hot tub, aware of his growing need.

Once immersed in the water, I turned to face Bruce, who was in the process of unbuttoning his jeans. My gaze roamed the length of his body as his jeans hit the deck revealing his tight black briefs. He showed no intimidation at my blatant inventory of his body, for he stepped boldly out of his briefs, which unleashed his swollen member.

He stepped into the water and took a position opposite me. I leaned close to him and saw his eyes widen fractionally as my nipples grazed his arm. I grabbed the bottle of wine and handed it to him. "Would you do the honors?"

He seemed aware of the game I was playing. He uncorked the bottle and placed it next to the glasses, then leaving the wine to breathe, he lit one candle. Like a hawk following its prey, I watched his every move. After lighting the second candle, he inched closer to me. He didn't blow out the match; instead he brought it close to my face, as if offering the small sacrifice of flame in worship of my beauty. But before I could blow it out, it burnt his finger. He yelped and flung the match.

"You like playing with fire or are you just trying to get me hot?" I asked, taking Bruce's burnt finger and placing it in my mouth. I closed my lips around his finger and began to move my tongue greedily all around. With gentle suction I drew it in and pulled it out, over and over, in and out. "Feel better?" I whispered softly. I knew that I was winning the game so far; I was a temptress, and he was certainly tempted.

"Wow," he muttered.

He moved across the tub, reached for the wine, poured us each a glass, then returned to my side. "Here's to the panties," he chuckled.

I raised my glass in a toast, then put it to my mouth, my tongue lightly licking the edge of the rim as the wine graced my palate. Together we sat, no words passing between us, watching each other.

I set my glass of wine down first. Purposefully I adjusted my position so that I slipped and my hand plunged into the water, conveniently landing on Bruce's enthusiastically throbbing sex.

He set down his glass as I began to rub his firmness, easing closer. My breasts rose to his full view, my hard nipples dusky rose peaks of desire. He brushed them gently with his fingers, seeming to revel in the feel of their silken tips, then traded his fingers for his entire hand. My body quivered with excitement and anticipation. With his right hand he began gliding his fingers along the side of my body, up and down, from my waist to my breasts, then back down my body again. He lightly massaged my back with his deft fingers, then finally nestled them inside the sensitive folds of my thighs.

Suddenly, our bodies set aflame with desire urged us forward. Bruce grabbed me by the hair and pulled me to him, placing his lips on mine in a deliberately claiming kiss. Our mouths opened, our tongues hungrily feasted on each other. Our ragged breathing grew synchronized, in perfect rhythm; almost as one, our pulses thrummed.

Bruce shifted his hands to my waist and, with a single motion, lifted me up to the side of the hot tub. Perched on the edge, my body opened to his zealous action. He kissed my calves, my knees, then rubbed his face against my thighs. His lips moved about my tender flesh, savoring the sweet scent of my sex. Easing himself against my body, he nibbled the hardened tips of my nipples; breathing heatedly and heavily on one, then the other. He laved my anguished buds with his tongue and suckled dotingly, giving each breast his absorbed attention, forcing me to release a strangled gasp.

He peered deep into my eyes and smiled just before his tongue slithered downward, venturing forth to find my hidden riches. Wickedly he bypassed my wet mound of desire, torturing me unmercifully, landing his attentions instead on my inner thighs. From thighs, to knee, to hipbone and back, he succulently kissed every inch of my flesh over and over, until I moved only by instinct. My innermost desires fed his. He was driving me to the edge of sexual insanity and back. Letting his tongue lay the pathway to my sweetness, he slowly, tauntingly, licked the outside of my pussy, then delved deep into the candied honey of my desire.

Finally ending my anguish, he rubbed his whiskered face against my tingling flesh and forged his supple tongue deep within the walls of my quivering cleft. Reacting to every one of his touches, I lost control, my body heaving and writhing under his amorous attention. He immersed the hood of my satin bulb within the warm cocoon of his mouth, sucking tenderly. Then he inserted two fingers deep within me, pressing upward, causing me to squirm uncontrollably. My muscles began contracting around him spasmodically. I teetered on the brink of sweet oblivion and as I forced his head closer to my unquenched sex my body flexed and orgasmic tension engulfed me. My back arched and my buttocks tightened. My pelvis pumped madly against the scalding rhythm of his tongue and his questing fingers. My hands searched for refuge. Letting go of his hair I grasped his muscular shoulders and my fingernails raked across his back. The sounds of my throes of passion instantly filled the air.

When my clenched fingers finally unfurled, Bruce licked his lips to draw the final vestiges of my sweet release into his mouth. He gently kissed his way back up my body, savoring the essence of my flesh. His amorous attention didn't stop until he nibbled on the lobe of my ear and whispered, "As hard as I am and as good as you taste, *I* have to wait until after dinner to have *my* dessert."

A little guilt-ridden, I thought momentarily about Sari and the grand introduction she had missed. However, filled with the sexual bliss of the past hour, I knew she would forgive me for sampling the sweetness of her neighbor. She would have her chance to unwrap Bruce when she returned.

I smiled dazedly as he turned, stepped up out of the tub and aided me to my feet. Once standing on steadfast legs he kissed my brow and said with a heartfelt sigh, "Welcome to the neighborhood."

CHAPTER 15

One brisk fall day as I awaited my plane's departure, I sipped a Hazelnut Latte' and read the Los Angeles Times. The front page headliner in the Arts and Leisure section caught my eye, "Tomorrow's Heart Holds Me Captive. A whimsical evening, a sensual touch, a desperate pleading—(310)555-1789. Local writer completely enamored by his Muse awaits her call to serve."

Finally, a newsworthy article, I thought wickedly as a coy smile crossed my lips. For in the midst of last summers travel I'd taken the opportunity to spend an evening wrapped in the arms of a beach god, on a moonlit seashore in Southern California. Although our verbal conversation hadn't been long, Geoff had disclosed that he wrote for a local paper and was always on the lookout for the next "big story". Our spoken words that evening had been few, yet our body language, our naked dueling in the darkness lasted for hours. And those hours would remain forever engraved in my mind and burnt into my soul

I settled back into the chair, closed my eyes, and as if I were still there with him, I watched the images project in slow motion. The remnants of salty air, the hunger in his kiss, the feel of his hot flesh pressed against mine. Well, here is how I remember Geoff and our brief interlude with sexual perfection.

Moonlit Stud

S itting alone on the back swing, I gazed out at the moon. I listened to the waves lapping against the shoreline and found myself suddenly yearning for the firm grasp of a man's hands pulling my hips tight against his growing desire. When the distant fog horn bellowed, an urge to take a midnight walk on the sandy cool beach beckoned me to stand and take action.

I left the swing in idle motion, and breathed a heavy sigh as the small wooden gate closed securely behind me and my bare feet melded with the sand. I looked in both directions, as if I were crossing a busy street; to the right I noticed a cool deserted beach, yet to the left of me sat a young, overtly handsome man, clad only in khaki surf shorts and tan, furry Ugg boots. His facial structure could have been carved in marble by Michelangelo: high, strong cheekbones, a five o'clock shadow that had creaped into our night, and long sandy brown hair that cradled his face. He appeared rugged, yet approachable. He had youth in his carefully crafted muscles and he reeked of sexuality. His rippled abs enticed me. Intoxicated by his aura, I found myself longing to feast upon every last inch of his elementally male form.

A rousing hunger surged through me as I began the quest to secure my prey. "Got an extra smoke," I inquired.

He looked up at me and without a word shook his pack and tapped a Marlboro Red out in my direction. He smiled as I reached out to accept the cigarette he offered. I touched his hand and a fiery sensation traveled from my fingertips to my toes within seconds, igniting every nerve ending along the way.

Briefly, I peeked back over my shoulder at the vacant swing on the porch. "Fuck it! If he didn't want me, this gorgeous morsel of a man would more than satisfy my thirst for affection." The temptation sitting just a few feet in front of me would not have to wait long to be swathed in the warmth of this temptress' touch.

I sat down opposite of him, to admire his youth. The night was warm, and as a gentle breeze brushed my cheek, I lifted the tobacco to my lips. Leaning in he cupped his hand around the flame of his lighter.

"Let me," he murmured in a throaty undertone.

I accepted his offering of flame and gently caressed the back his hand. I watched as he nestled back into his chair, buried in the sand, and sat in silence as I memorized every bronzable curve of his face. The backlighting from the porch added a sensory heightening hue. His eyes locked with mine halting me from savoring the moment. I was awestruck, for the first time in many moons.

"You thirsty?" he asked.

"I am," I replied.

"Beer or a bottle of wine? What I have is yours for the taking."

"Is your girlfriend waiting inside?" I inquired.

"Not tonight."

"Then a beer would be great," I replied, a fiendish grin gracing my lips.

He rose and sauntered into the house. Within a few minutes, he returned with beer in hand. We talked, for what seemed to be an eternity. My mind was not on the conversation, but rather what pleasures he was capable of performing upon my willing and daring body. I yearned to touch him, to set his manhood free and measure its length within the moist, warm, enclosures of my mouth. I wanted to taste him, to graze my fingernails across his unyielding ass, while I teased the tiny fissure at the tip of his dick with my limber tongue.

I can't remember what we discussed, for my mind was elsewhere. However, when he drifted towards me and leaned down, turning my face to his with a gentle pull of my cheek, and kissed me…I realized that my burning thoughts were now going to become actions.

His lips were full and soft and when they melded with my own, a lustful craving stirred from deep within. Our tongues danced. His lips searched my warm skin, first kissing my cheek, my ear, and then the nape of my neck. Almost as if he were a vampire he bit down on the tender bridge of flesh between my neck and shoulder and exhaled a deep sigh of hunger. I allowed his gifted mouth to ravish my body as I became a willing captive to his charms; one who desired no rescue until completely satisfied.

Eagerly, I grabbed the back of his muscular shoulders, attempting to clutch him snugly to me. But before I could quench my urge, he pulled back and retreated to his chair, leaving me breathless and aching for more.

"If I'd seen you earlier, you'd still be in my bedroom," he murmured, sitting down, licking his lips as if to savor the taste of me. Slowly, tauntingly, he lifted his beer to clear his palate, cooling the obvious heat that our sexually charged confrontation had kindled.

Our tête-à-tête had begun. I leaned back in the sand and wallowed in a passion filled haze. Dressed in a pair of azure blue Victoria Secret booty shorts and a matching tank, my full breasts peaked and my nipples stood at attention, begging to be touched. My feet were bare and I wore no panties. Needless to say, I yearned for release and my penchant for recklessness had led me to checkmate. I, being the queen, fancied to take the king down.

"What are you thinking?" he asked.

"Honestly, I was wondering what name I should cry out when you set my body aflame and leave me burgeoning on climax?"

"Hmm. My name is Geoff. And if you're calling out my name, then the night hasn't ended as I'd hoped. You see, I prefer it when my women scream out in wild ecstasy without worrying who I am. In all reality, I crave nothing more than to be a slave to your every sexual fantasy."

With a wink, he rose once again and retreated to the house. He returned, holding two beers, one of which he handed to me. I held it tightly within my grip as he twisted the cap off for me then took a seat straddling me from behind on the sand, nestling his body to mine. A strangled gasp lodged in my throat when his steely hardness began to pulse against the flimsy covering of my booty shorts. Attempting to reduce my sexual craving I took a strong guzzle of my beer then twisted the bottle into the sand.

Intuitively Geoff began a seductive quest, stimulating every inch of my flesh once again; first kissing the back of my bared shoulders where his mouth searched and his tongue flicked. His hands lightly grazed my arms, shoulders, and then finally found sanctuary on my firm breasts where he gently began a sensual massage. A light squeeze, then a firm fondle, all the while moaning hot and heavy. I watched, entranced, as his fingers began to trace spiraling patterns over my breasts drawing ever closer to my bereft nipples, stoking my flame. My thighs tensed as every slow circle enlivened my senses. Finally Geoff pinched the tight, aching buds with just enough pressure to whet my precarious appetite.

"I want you," he purred into my ear.

"Not here," I said motioning to the house next door.

"I'll be right back," he said, rising, and then disappearing into his house once again. He returned with a blanket draped over his shoulder, held out a hand to me, and murmured provocatively, "Let's walk."

I took his hand as he helped me to my feet. I was fearless. I longed to be lured to the dark side of temptation. Geoff wanted me and from this point forward there was no turning back. When I stood, he hastily wrapped his arms around me and once again he kissed me with those mouthwatering, full lips. His desire was apparent and I could no longer resist reaching down to stroke his growing length through his shorts. He was hard—huge—and evidently hungry for me.

A sensor light flashed from the porch next door and I ducked, burying my face in Geoff's chest. He motioned forward and as we began walking towards the shoreline I reveled in the play of the silver moonlight shadowing across his rippled abs. Without speaking we walked, hand in hand, while the music of the sea surrounded us.

When the lifeguard station filtered into view, Geoff pulled me to him. Peering intensely into my eyes he tilted my chin towards him, kissing me full and passionately; his hands beginning to roam relentlessly. Slowly, he slid one hand down the front of my shorts and the other down the back. Geoff's fingers began an intimate sequestering of the private realms of my innermost desire.

His fingers became instruments, playing their own tune as they searched out the velvety path that led to the hood of my sex. With his left hand he inserted one finger, and then two, into my moistened shell where fantasy filled fluids coated his dexterous digits. With his right hand he began to stimulate the outer lining of the taut skin shielding the entrance to my shaded recess, awakening the sequestered animal within me. My fearless nature became fueled by outward desire and I was not going to stop as I swayed only inches away from sweet oblivion. With his fingers questing, I found myself shimmering in a mist of sweat as my intimate walls exploded in bliss and a natural liquid glide aroused a hunger from depths unknown.

"You're a naughty bitch aren't you?" Geoff murmured in my ear.

"Naughty or nice, I want you naked," I cried. "So, quit playing around and fuck me!"

Geoff's energetic advances didn't stop. In a rhythm all his own he managed to stimulate both alcoves of my body, impelling deeper and faster. I became dizzy as his sweet torment forced me to grab the stiff up-thrust of his sex and squeeze tightly as my body, in a state bordering on frantic, gave way to the pure pleasure of multiple orgasms.

Boneless under the strong hold of Geoff, I managed to regain my composure. My nimble fingers untied the string holding his surf shorts up. Without hesitation he stepped out of the fabric and brushed his hardened cock against the lightweight material covering my burning flesh. His brawny arms pulled me against his Herculean chest. He rocked his hips deliberately, enticing me into another frenzied state. Then as quickly as he had pulled my body to his, he pushed me back.

My breath caught as he dropped to his knees before me in supplication. I became his altar and his mouth, perfectly lined up with my breasts, opened for worship. I gazed down at him and closed my eyes tight, feeling as though I were about to combust as he pulled the straps of my tank top over my shoulders and down to my waist.

"Too tired to continue?" he inquired.

"Never," I replied. "Just need a minute to un-cloud my rose-colored glasses."

"No time to rest. I got the feeling you wanted a real man? A real man doesn't rest when a brazen beauty graces his presence."

My shirt rested on my hips and Geoff's supple, moistened lips began to tease my left breast as his hand caressed my right breast. Softly, he bit the tip of my nipple, and then drew the hardened bud into his heated mouth. My legs began to tremble.

"Mmmm," he moaned against my flesh.

As his tongue traveled from my chest down to the edge of my waistline I shivered with a hint of naughty delight. While I anticipated his next move I enjoyed the feeling of his strong hands resting on my hipbones. Before I knew it, he stripped me bare in one swift, well rehearsed motion. I stood naked, unveiled in the moonlight, a cool and brisk sea breeze whispered against my ass, leaving me breathless and awestruck.

Geoff gestured for me to lie down on the blanket. I obeyed willingly and smiled as he knelt down, straddling me.

Tenderly he began to caress my body. First my neck, then my breasts, my stomach, my inner thighs and my calves. He purposefully bypassed the nestle of curls which hid my flaming desire. My body writhed instinctively beneath him. Desperately I wanted to feel him surge deep inside me. Affectionately Geoff inserted two long and nimble fingers into my well lubricated sheath. Once again my body became his personal altar that I'd allow him to worship at for as long as he so desired.

Geoff didn't remove his fingers, as his mouth sought out the center of my need. His tongue danced upon my clit as his fingers quested within the core of my being. Having already succumbed to his persuasive mastery of the art of seduction, I wanted to hold out. I hoped to enjoy the pleasure of his personal attack for hours. However, my body defied me, unleashing climactic ecstasy once again. I reached up and pulled Geoff's curly locks tight within my fingers as the silken friction of our bodies left me hazed with passion.

"Oh, don't stop. Oh yeah. Oh...ummm," I cried.

Once my eyes fluttered open, Geoff asked, "You don't think we're finished do you?"

"Hell no!" I replied. "You awakened my sleeping goddess. I hope you're prepared!"

"If I'm not, I'm sure you'll educate me." He lay down next to me on the blanket and instructed me to get on top.

I knew he wanted me to face him, but now I wanted the control. I straddled him, with my ass facing him. I had more dominance this way. I lifted myself up and spread my cresting beauty with my left fingers and with my right hand I stroked his hard dick, which pulsed with ridges of blood filled veins. I positioned his cock at the entrance of my swollen, needy, core. I enticed him, tantalizingly, by rubbing the tip of his steel rod against my already wet pussy, eager to please him, yet longing to tempt him. Insatiably, I sat down slowly, allowing him to feel every inch of me close around him.

He forcefully grabbed onto my hips and I knew I held him captive. I sat firmly against his hip bones and allowed him the reins to move my body any way he wanted. Aspiring to drive him over the edge I began to caress his balls with my left hand and then skillfully ran my nails along the side of his ass.

"Spank me," I gasped, lifting up off his silken snake in smooth cadence, squeezing him within the walls of my tight sheath, and then thrusting myself back down against his upraised hips.

Temptingly I slid my right hand into personal self pleasuring mode and eased my thumb and middle finger around the base of his cock. Every time I eased up off him I squeezed his dick within my clutch giving the added attention needed to force him to cum.

Geoff's moans grew heavy and his spankings swifter and more discordant. His hips began to gyrate. His once fluid and rhythmic motions became harried and I found myself being lifted up and thrust hard back down on top of him. Geoff had become an animal in rut and I his ultimate release.

"Fuck yeah!" he hollered gutturally into the night air. "Oh, you sexy bitch! Don't stop. Oh yeah!"

He held my ass tight to him as his body slowed in motion and he pulled back, milking the final remnants of his seed from his spent pecker. As his grip loosed on my hips he lifted his hands to my shoulders where he slowly began to caress my back. Tentatively he grazed his fingers along the side of my ribcage, and then across the bridge of my ass. He carefully lifted me up off him and drew me in close. As I lay next to him in silence I found myself comfortable in the circle of his arms and rested until our breathing returned to normal.

A light in the distance forced us to rise from our contented state and quickly find our clothes in an attempt to regain the appearance of decency. Within moments a beach patrol officer pulled up next to where our sexual escapade had played out.

"Beach is closed," he intoned.

"Yeah, but I live right there," Geoff replied gesturing back.

"Doesn't matter. Rules are rules."

"You got it. We're on our way."

"Be careful."

"Always."

Geoff took me by the hand and together we walked across the beach, toward the wooden gate which held the reality of a cold and lonely bed.

"Your girlfriend's one lucky girl, Geoff. If you'd quit cheating on her, that is."

"Oh, my lady. You were far too tempting to resist. And, if given the chance, I'd do it all over again."

He brushed the hair away from my face affectionately and kissed me gently on the cheek. Then as if in desperation, he drew me close, wrapped me in his strong arms and held me to his firm chest. When he finally loosened his embrace, he kissed me once more on the mouth, like it was the last time he would ever be kissed. Our tongues twined in a familiar tango and my ferocity, having been unleashed near the tides, voraciously returned. Once more, in Geoff's arms, the incandescent fire stirred. Savoring his touch, I pined for his kiss, praying it would never end. Our lips did part though, and as quickly as our dynamic duel had begun, it came to a standstill.

Standing on my tiptoes I hugged him, clutching him tightly. Huskily I breathed into his ear, "Thank you for worshipping my body this evening. You truly quenched my thirst for sexual exploration." Then, softly I cradled his whiskery, chiseled face within my hands. I kissed him once more, drawing his bottom lip into my mouth, then released him and turned back towards the gate. His smoldering gaze burned against my backside, but I couldn't turn around. My resistance was low and I was *always* hungry for more.

"Dear lady, what's your name?" Geoff called out to me.

"Tomorrow," I said. "There's always tomorrow."

"May I see you in the morning? Columbian coffee and total body rub-downs are my specialty."

I was seductively silent.

"Tomorrow, then?" he asked, almost pleadingly.

I knew that I'd be gone before he had awakened, for the house and the man behind the wooden gate no longer held my heart, nor my interest. My beach front liberation freed my recent inhibitions, reminding me that life was meant to be lived and way to short to spend it with someone whose eyes could not see my worth. Tomorrow I would fly away to an unknown and hope-filled destiny.

Taking another sip of my latte, I brought myself back to the present, aware again of the bustling airport. I smiled knowingly, for as I had told Geoff, "Tomorrow, there's always tomorrow."

I didn't need to finish his article for the cast of characters were alive and real. I knew the woman. I knew the man who wrote the words. I had thoroughly enjoyed the experience and the memory would forever remain ingrained in my mind and worthy of print.

CHAPTER 16

Deep and meaningful discussions between my brother and I were always about relationships. One night over a bottle of Merlot he'd insisted that I should be the first to settle down and get hitched. Well, well, well, the salty sea air from which I'd just returned had definitely freed me from giving my brother's request any afterthought. The dreamy warm location near the equator had cleansed my palate of relationship worry and kicked my penchant for naughtiness into high gear. While vacationing I'd sequestered two mesmerizing beauties, and shared the temptations of my worldly wiles, and learned a few things hidden behind the closed doors of cloak-and-dagger.

As I pushed open the door of home, I did so through a months worth of unopened mail. Carefully, I moved the postal droppings from the floor, to the table top where a bubble wrapped package from distant lands caught my eye. The return address—Cancun Mexico.

Intrigued, I withdrew a pair of scissors from the drawer and cut into the package. I retrieved a VHS tape which was hidden within the popcorn filling in addition to a letter which was taped to the back of it.

Curiosity overwhelmed me, but before watching the video I opened the letter. My jaw dropped and a delighted giggle rose from my throat, "Annie, you naughty bitch. I wonder just how much of our time together you captured?"

I gleefully walked over to my big wingback chair and took a seat. Pulling my knees to my chest I began to reminisce about my travels and the women who challenged my spirit for a while.

Tropical Torment

Once the trip had been paid for I'd had second thoughts about traveling alone. It was my desire to take a companion, yet none of my favorites were available for such a long holiday, especially over the Christmas season. My momentary doubts receded as I gazed out my window on the 18th floor at the beautifully tanned forms below.

In addition to a fully loaded suitcase, I had also packed my eye candy. Chameleon eye lenses: Hazel, Brown, Green, Lavender and Blue. I had a bikini for every day of travel and decided that my eyes would dress the color as well.

Bryson, my stylist, had skillfully fashioned multi-colored highlights throughout my dark locks and the sun kissed the caramel blonde shades just so, adding warmth that hopefully no one could resist running their fingers through.

I carefully chose aqua-green Brazilian cut bottoms and a stark white halter-top to accentuate my dark skin for my first trip poolside. As my scantily clad form posed statuesque in front of the large bay window, I found myself eager for an adventurous voyeur to watch me; secretly desiring to ravage me for lunch as I prepared to descend to the pool.

Slowly, I turned from the window, twisted my hair up into a loose bun atop my head, grabbed my bag and headed out the door to the elevators which took me straight down to the pool. The intoxicating smell of coconuts filled my senses as I sauntered past dozens of bared bodies; gloriously stretched out, on the cobalt blue chaise lounge chairs, worshiping the sun goddess. The array of tiny fabric swatches providing the barest protection to sensitive parts of the body mesmerized me. Pervasive colors: every hue—every shade—contrasted individual body shape and size. Before I had a chance to lie down on my towel and lube myself with coconut oil, a cabaña boy appeared next to me.

"Would you like a drink?"

Coyly I looked up, a smile crossed my lips and I responded, "What do you drink?"

"Pineapple Daiquiris Senorita," he replied then winked at me.

"That would be perfect," I replied as he turned and rushed off to fulfill my request.

I slid my sun glasses down the bridge of nose so I could watch the people watchers. Entranced, I picked up my bottle of Hawaiian Tropic and began to spritz my body from the tips of my flowered adorned toenails to the tips of my plump, ripe breasts.

The cabaña boy returned before I had finished my personal body massage and as I put the cap back on the spray bottle, he placed my drink on the table between the lounge chairs. I handed him a very generous tip that would assure me speedy personal assistance for future libations.

"Gracias, Senorita. My name is Carlos. If you need anything let me know and I will be at your service." He flashed me a smile, then quickly turned and rushed to his next customer.

He was tall and his body rippled with cord-like muscles. Although a young man of Mexican heritage, he exuded the sexuality of a young Hercules. I licked my lips in outward desire, but knew it was far too soon to begin attacking the locals—especially those within the walls of the hotel. I fought the urge to tempt him. My first conquest had to be monumental. This was *my* trip and I'd start it off with a bang. Once ignited, the days and nights would only get better.

I needed a fellow traveler—someone who wouldn't shy away from the sexual world that I'd enjoyed for so long. Maybe a tryst with a couple; one man and one woman, two to please me. Or perhaps two delectable and most definitely daring women.

It seemed like hours before I located the perfect prospects. In all actuality it was only an hour and five pineapple daiquiris later. Just enough time and the right amount of liquor in the watered down complimentary drinks to have caught a good buzz when a lusciously ripe female couple floated towards me.

I knew in an instant that they were more than just friends. Friends didn't walk that close. And these tempting beauties bodies were almost touching; touching in a sexually teasing manner—not by accident but by choice and desire. My stomach fluttered. My thighs began to quiver and my heart raced as I anticipated them sitting in the empty chairs next to me. As you might have guessed, I've had trysts with women lovers and I found myself quickly captivated, like a fly in a web—prey waiting to be devoured.

I became the voyeur I'd desired earlier and I didn't mind watching them flirt with one another. I wanted to obtain them for my own gratification, and yet I wanted to pleasure them at the same time. I would begin by...

"Are you saving these seats for someone?"

"Unbelievable," I sighed.

"Excuse me?"

"Hmm. Sorry. I was just thinking out loud. The seats are empty and you're welcome to them. I'm just exceptionally glad that you aren't some slovenly drunk man hoping for a quickie."

"Nope. Last time I checked I didn't have a dick. I'm Samantha and this is my girlfriend Annie."

Smiling up at them both I replied, "Camille—but you can call me Cami."

Annie was fair skinned, auburn hair and eyes a smoky hue of gray. Her petite frame graced the tight string bikini that she sported. Her partner Samantha had long flowing locks of ebony, with the greenest eyes I'd ever seen. Those eyes sparkled like crystallized emeralds bewitching me. I'd be putty in her hands if she reached out to touch me. If she locked eyes with me I'd not be able to stop myself from drawing her into my arms and kissing her deeply upon her full luscious lips, shining with a drizzle of pink satin gloss.

I would pull her athletic frame against me and press my flesh to hers. Our breasts would graze—our nipples forming erect peaks of desire that would unleash the wild nature of our primal being.

I licked my lips to moisten them. My breath caught as Sam's round buttocks appeared firm and flawless, inches from me. Her tan line lay secretly hidden beneath the tiny fabric of her thong as sprays of fringe waved across her bare ass, imploring my molten stare to linger. Her toned stomach was accented by the rope belt of her suit bottom and her youthful breasts filled her top in a tear drop form. Men are not the only ones who think that nothing beats the soft, warm, natural feeling of a woman's breast pressed against one's skin. Looking at Sam made me yearn for the silken sheets on my hotel bed with her lying next to me awaiting my tender touch.

Sam seductively toyed with the tie on the back of her flaming red suit top. The delicate white flowers embossed on the fabric seemed to dance when her fingers moved and began to trace the bottom outline below her breasts. I couldn't help my blatant ogling. My eyes were locked on her and she knew that she held me captive. My smoldering scrutiny of her body caught the attention of Annie who instantly began to giggle.

"Don't worry Cami, she won't bite, but she may nibble," she stated matter a fact.

"A little erotic pleasure never hurt anyone, did it?" I inquired.

"Can't say that it ever hurt me," Sam replied. "Was that an invitation?"

"Sounded like it to me," Annie replied.

"I think that our sexual tête-à-tête will lead to my further temptation, however, I'd like to be bathed by the sun's kiss for a while. I'll need more vitamin D to keep up with a pair as enticing as you. I'm up for the challenge, but being too eager won't allow everyone to get their juices flowing."

"Oh, I see," said Annie. "You're going to make us wait? I hope you brought something to cool you down, cuz I really like to have people watch."

With that, Annie began to lightly tickle Sam's bared stomach: she traced tiny circles, and then floated her French manicured fingertips around the entire outline of her bikini as the tiny white flowers seemed to shimmer in the sunlight beneath her touch. Her careful tormenting didn't stop here. She began to roam across the velvety flesh along the inseam of Sam's thighs. At this point I raised my drink to my lips in order to stop myself from interrupting their private performance. It had become outwardly apparent to me that Annie was a crafted lover and she had every intention of making my sun-bathing ritual an excuse to tease me. A just reminder that the upcoming pleasure that would be bestowed on all parties involved would be well worth it, no matter who took the lead.

Knowing that this exhibition would end with everyone satisfied, I breathlessly watched as Annie slipped her delicate, long fingers beneath the front edge of Sam's bikini bottom... revealing to me a glimpse of darkened curls. She did this with such skill, that I found myself a fully captivated audience to their sexual display. Sam's body turned towards Annie slightly to meet her touch as the muscles along her inner thighs began to flex with each movement Annie's fingers made. Sam shifted her left leg upwards, exposing her ass to me and showcasing Annie's quest into her most vulnerable recesses. With her leg moved I had gained visible access to the show. The bikini fabric had been moved over just enough to allow Annie the most mobility with her dexterous fingers.

I was the voyeur, watching as Sam's ass tightened each time Annie's fingers delved into her. Tauntingly, Annie slid her fingers in and out of Sam's intimate channel; three times. Then she would wait with her fingertips just at the outer edge of Sam's sweet lips, teasingly allowing them to slowly glide back into her. I could tell that Sam was burgeoning on the edge of full submission as her thighs began to quiver.

A hint of naughtiness overcame me and my urge to trade places with Annie created a sublime desire within my loins. I couldn't allow Annie to enjoy this luscious creature any further. I was used to being the one in charge of the sexual play, so I made the decision not to take a back seat to this encounter. I wanted to see Sam's flesh bared to me. I needed to have her naked...exposed...ready to be worshipped and adored. I wanted to taste the subtle musk of her sex and tease her with my tongue until she begged me to consume her entirely.

I sat up, moved my legs near Sam's ass and stood up. I leaned over and whispered lightly into her ear, "I'm ready to feast upon your lovely body and worship you the way you deserve." Then, I looked to Annie who still had her fingers dancing within Sam's sex, "Is it alright with you if I steal your girlfriend for a while?"

"Why? Did the show get to you?" she asked.

"Not the show, the participants. I promise to have her back to you within the next few hours."

"Sam makes her own decisions. You should have sensed that by now. Maybe we can all have dessert this evening at 8:00? Our room number is 1705." Having said that, Annie briskly removed her probing fingers and sat up. She rose, took two steps towards the pool and dove in. When she surfaced, she called back to Sam, "Don't do anything I wouldn't do and have fun."

Sam stood up and reached out to me. She took me by the hand and without saying a word, walked with me away from the poolside, towards the elevator.

The elevator was glass and you could see the entire seascape once you reached any floor above 2, however, anyone looking in from the outside couldn't see in. The inside of the elevator was lined entirely with mirror, an added bonus for the vain and wardrobe challenged.

Once those doors had closed us in, Sam gracefully approached me. I am used to being the aggressor, but here I felt out of place. This time I was the prey. Softly Sam touched my cheeks and turned my face to hers. Her lips brushed against mine and instantly set my blood on fire. I reached out spontaneously and drew her to me. As if we had known each other for years our tongues eagerly glided into one another's mouths. We were dancing to our own rhythm and my senses stirred with an insufferable urgency. Just then the elevator stopped.

"The women's locker room in the gym has a wonderful double-headed steam shower, built perfectly for two," Sam intoned.

I couldn't respond. My arousal trickled from my sex. I anxiously followed her in silence, listening to the tap of her sandals on the marble floor. Down the softly lit hallway we walked with the thumping of my heart pounding in my chest as the gym came into view.

Sam adoringly took me by the hand. All eyes were upon us as we ventured from the packed work out room into the locker room. Fortunately the shower area was vacant.

The room was adorned with beautiful mosaic tiles, bright colors flowed from floor to ceiling. Pinks the color of the sunset—blue as cool as the morning sky—yellow as bright as the local flowering orchids.

Sam turned leisurely around and placed her thumbs inside the outer edge of her thong. "God I wish I had a camera to capture your beauty," I murmured throatily.

Sam turned her head slightly and caught my enamored gaze. An array of color surrounded her, framing her, almost as if she were a posing artist's model. Seductively she bent forward, legs slightly apart and stripped out of her bottoms. Her bronzed buttocks encased the full beauty of her alluring pussy, which she purposefully allowed me to view in all its glory as she held her position, seducing me.

Sam's skin was flawless: tanned, sleek, and hairless. Hairless that is, except for the small narrow line of clipped dark curls which showcased her luscious haven like a landing strip for my tongue. Arched over in front of me, she unveiled her sexual flower, the petals gently unfurling.

My legs quivered and my stomach fluttered. God, how I wanted to kneel down and kiss her secret pleasures, delivering upon her sexual button the most gracious spanking with my tongue.

Standing in front of me provocatively, Sam reached behind her back and untied the string that secured her suit top to her body. I watched breathlessly as her breasts came in full view and her pink nipples instantly hardened, puckering as the cool air in the room caressed them. She knew how she tormented me with her erotic strip tease, yet she continued without haste and tossed her top to me.

I needed no striptease to please her. The fact that I wanted her was more than apparent. I disrobed and followed her into the shower. Sam had been right, the shower was perfect for two. Large, smooth rocks were stacked at each end of the bench which resembled makeshift chairs in a water fall. Wantonly, I secured the stained glass doors behind me.

I didn't wait for Sam to give me a signal. I approached her slowly and reached out, cupping her breasts. Her breath caught as my fingers softly massaged her budding nipples. One by one I withdrew my fingers from her chest and placed them into my mouth and wetted them. Tantalizingly I repositioned my moistened fingertips back upon her nipples, supplying an added friction to my actions. While engaging in finger play with Sam's nipples I moved towards her until our skin almost touched. At this juncture she leaned in, her lips fusing with mine and instantly, pleasuring her was all I was about. I dropped my hands and gradually pushed apart her thighs. My thumb gently began rubbing her clit as my fingers probed for entrance between her slick, soft lips.

Sam's kiss became more demanding and her tongue traced patterns around my own as she grabbed my ass and pulled me to her. Our breasts touched. Our mouths searched.

Instinctively Sam lifted her leg atop one of the smooth rocks and began to writhe beneath my fingers as they quested relentlessly within her. Being the bold lover that I am I wanted to test my limits; leaving my one hand with searching fingers inside her pussy, I moved the other around the back of her ass and gently began caressing the outer limits of her tender anus, utilizing the natural lubrication already flowing from her.

Sam didn't seem to mind as I began to initiate a tender entrance into her tight sheath. Actually, her body began to gyrate in a rocking motion, all the while holding firm against my nakedness as both my hands worked in unremitting unison.

Kissing is a more intimate action than sexual penetration. Knowing that a kiss could make or break any sexual encounter, I seductively drew Sam's tongue within my mouth and suckled it. I grazed my teeth gently against it, pulling her tender flesh into mine, making us one. I wanted her to come, writhing in cataclysmic ecstasy. And as my hands drew her dampened entrances towards climax, I adorned her tongue, her lips, and her mouth, with lustful affection.

Just as Sam's body tightened and flexed beneath my touch, she pulled away from me. Bedazzled, I couldn't force myself to stop my advances. "Lay down," I instructed, with a hint of desperation. "Let me finish pleasuring you."

"No." she replied a little too quickly. "I want to feel you beneath me."

"Bossy aren't we?" I intoned.

"Not bossy. I just know what I want. Now lie back and let me quench your sexual appetite."

At that minute I had to admit that it was a welcome and unexpected pleasure to have Sam being the dominating force. I lay down without delay on the warm, moist, bench. My full breasts slid to form and my thighs slightly parted with hopeful excitement. Sam reached up and turned on the water, aiming the stream purposefully at the small, downy patch of hair that decorated the feminine folds between my thighs. The constant pulse of water beat against the crest of my clit, and a fine mist coated my flesh. With a shiver of delight, I drew in a quick, fluttering breath filled with the gleeful enthusiasm of a child alone in Willy Wonka's Candy Store.

Within moments my fervor was gratified as Sam knelt down and positioned herself; leaning over my hips allowing her nipples to graze against my thighs, producing an instant rush of my womanly flavors. As the steamy, hot, water pulsed against my flesh Sam began caressing my center of desire with her right index finger. Calculatingly, she leaned forward and blew a long, heated breath against the upper crest of my neatly trimmed hairline. The warmth from her breath set alight my flesh and I tingled throughout my body, craving her further advances. I closed my eyes and took hold of the side boards of the bench; waiting, wondering, hoping.

"Oh, God," I moaned as my torturous wait was finally over.

The warmth of Sam's tongue bathed my clit. First she began with tiny delicate arcs. A few flicks with the tip of her tongue and then she began to devour the very bosom of my innermost passage. Her tongue turned from the softness of a newly discovered passion to the desperate need of addict as it forged deep within the demanding recess of my clenching pussy. Adding further friction to the blissful torment she was delivering upon my sex, Sam inserted her index and middle fingers within my feminine folds. While I teetered on the edge, on the brink of climax, Sam offered no ready submission. Her tongue continued its mission to please me; her fingers searched, her mouth suckled, and her tongue quested my intimate depths.

Like most, I hate to party alone. But more than that, I definitely hate to come alone. So, as Sam's moans against my clit compelled me to reach out and entwine my fingers in her tousled, wet locks, I pulled her from my bed of delight and forced her to meet my lust filled gaze.

"Straddle my face," I insisted.

Sam uttered no words. She delved back into my feminine feast and without losing a lick hoisted herself upon the bench and placed her smooth thighs on either side of my head. I inhaled her womanly scent as I parted her swollen folds with my tongue. I raised my left hand and playfully spanked her tight ass. With my right hand I began to gently stroke her kernel of passion, as my tongue slid easily into the puckering of her taunt ass. I reamed her star of wonder with my tongue, aggressively matching every stroking motion my fingers made within her tight pussy.

The cadence of our lovemaking liaison mimicked that of a couple who had been together for years. We knew what the other needed and desired as if telepathic. My back arched and my ass tightened under her personal attack. Together we met each others every flex and gyration.

I rubbed and kneaded her ass with my hand. I massaged her, as my fingers tempted both avenues of her open and inviting channels. Her ass tightened within my grasp and as the thrusting motions of my hips became harried, Sam's devotion to my clit forced my body to release. As I came I felt the warmth of her climax flow against my fingers. We had become one, climaxing together.

Lying exhausted and sexually spent, Sam slid to my side, pillowing her head against my calves as she began to tickle my legs with her nails. Languorously gazing at me like a kitten in a pool of sunshine she murmured, "I knew you'd be great the moment you began erotically rubbing your body with coconut oil."

"Oh really," I responded, my smile filled with satisfaction. "And what about you? Standing there in the sun, swaying your hips, titillating me with that beautiful ass of yours?"

"Oh you know that show was for Annie."

"Uh-huh. That's why she was turned the other way, lying on her towel."

"Okay. So we were both interested. We're both thrill-seekers. And we both put the flirting to bed."

"What do you think Annie will say?"

"Did you tape it?" Sam replied.

"Hmm, why didn't we think of that?" I said with a chuckle, resting my hand on her ass, lingering in the warmth of the water, and the mist of sexual satisfaction.

Needless to say, Sam had been the highlight of my stay at that resort. Together we'd taken the bonds of sisterhood to a new level. With a wicked smile, I once again opened the letter I'd received and read the following:

"Senorita Camille,

Please be advised that I received a security report in great detail about an afternoon interlude you and your friend experienced in our spa shower. We are grateful that you felt comfortable in our hotel, however, the surveillance cameras are on 24/7 for the protection of our guests. Moving these cameras negates this protection and we ask that in the future you refrain from repositioning them. I'm enclosing the remarkable video taken. No copies were made and the cameras have been returned to their normal station, so as other couples may enjoy the pleasures such as you had without receiving a letter from me. You're truly a beautiful woman, Senorita Camille. If you require further personal attention during your next stay, please don't hesitate to phone me personally.

Ramon Jose/Head of Security"

Reading this letter in its entirety left me wanting. If the tape contains what the letter says it does, my afternoon would be filled with multiple pleasures, watching Sam in all her glory, satisfy me once again.

CHAPTER 17

I must assert that to be the object of someone's impassioned desire incites my loins to tingle with intrepid excitement. One glorious Saturday morning as the sun beamed down lighting the beach in a luminous glitter, my cell phone began buzzing across the counter, alerting me to a text message.

My eyes were drawn from the view and I perused the text message from a friend in Washington State, "Darling, my boat will rock you all the way to heaven if you come quickly! Awaiting your arrival, Dylan."

These words coursed over and over in my mind and I found myself overwhelmed with a whimsical, girlish titillation which impelled me to drop everything, pack lightly, and hail a cab to the airport.

After two years of wondering "what if," a missed opportunity had finally come full circle and I'd be damned if I'd wonder any longer. My journey back to the Pacific Northwest would end with me cradled in the arms of my modern day Poseidon; regardless of inclement weather, the waves would bow to my will.

The Captain's "Captive" Mate

I pushed through the crowded corridors of SeaTac Airport. To my surprise, instead of having to fight my way to the car rental counter, a uniformed man held aloft a sign, "Darlin' come be my first mate," Dylan.

"I do believe that you're my ride," I stated tongue in cheek as I approached the driver.

"How was your flight?" he asked taking my bag and motioning for me to follow him.

"Very relaxing. Thank you for asking," I replied as we walked to the car where he opened the door, then turned to me extending his hand to help me in.

While he placed my bag in the trunk, I settled into the back seat, my stomach fluttering. Within moments, the window divider slid down. The driver turned to me and smiled. "My name's John and I'll be escorting you to the marina where Dylan's waiting. He wanted me to give you this once we were on our way."

I held out my hands and took the elaborately wrapped package from John. Before I could inquire as to the nature of the gift, the window closed and I was left alone. I sat for a moment, trying to decide whether I should open the gift immediately or wait until we reached the dock.

John's voice chimed in through the speakers and interrupted my thoughts, "There's a chilled bottle of wine in the fridge, uncorked, ready for you to treat yourself. Grab a glass and top it off. Then unwrap your gift and let me know what my brother bought you."

"Brothers—hmm—maybe later," I purred from the back of my throat as I slid across the seat, opened the fridge and carefully poured myself some wine. I lifted the crystal goblet to my lips and took a sip of the crisp, sweet libation. I cautiously set my fragile tumbler on the arm rest between the seats and pulled the ribbon from the package.

The wrapping paper tore easily and once discarded, a beautiful buckskin hat box came into view. I lifted off the top. Inside laid a bright navy blue bikini, a crimson sarong, and a stark white captain's hat.

"Hey, John. Are we going to be able to stop somewhere so I can change into the wonderfully captivating outfit your brother procured for me?" I asked as a saucy smile once again graced my lips.

"There's a beautifully plush ladies' lounge at the yacht club. We should be there in about 20 minutes. Just sit back, relax, and savor your wine."

Instead of issuing a reply, I leaned back, sipped my wine and envisioned how Dylan was going to look illuminated by the bright sunshine. To say the least, I was more than anxious to greet him properly. It had been two years since I'd last seen him. The time we had planned to spend together had been suspended by an urgent overseas business matter which Dylan had been called to tend to. Our romantic weekend touring the San Juan Islands, wrapped in the erotic throes of passion, had been squelched when the reality of normal life had reared its ugly head.

Now, just minutes from seeing Dylan again, I recalled how his magnificent eyes had bewitched me, body and soul, from the first moment I'd gazed into them. His hazel eyes, seemingly speckled with a hue of honey, surrounding the mesmerizing emerald green iris, had left me spellbound. He'd been wearing a deep green t-shirt and warn, denim jeans the day he'd assisted me off the party barge and onto the floating dock. His dark wavy hair slicked back, and a small twist of curls dangled across his forehead accentuating his strong chiseled cheek bones, which made my heart palpitate. The once over I'd given him was only enough to whet my appetite. I continued my scrutiny of his body as I viewed his bronze skin glistening in the sun and I knew I was hooked. The first few moments I'd spent suspended in time, dreaming of his body pressed firmly against mine, imagining rocking with him in waves of impassioned desire.

The car slowed and as the engine idled my loins began to quiver with a tingling craving. Once again the divider lowered and John stated matter a fact, "Your captain awaits, my lady."

I gathered my purse and the contents of my package just as John opened the door and extended a hand to me. "You'll find a young woman inside, her name's Nancy and she'll direct you to my brother's boat. Have a wonderful time."

"I'm hoping to, John. You wouldn't happen to have a business card for me? You know, just in case I need a ride in the future?"

Smiling, John reached into his lapel and retrieved a black and silver card. "If ever you need a ride..." he paused and meaningfully cast his gaze over my body, "I'll be right there."

"Thank you," I said with a knowing smile, then turned and sauntered into the building.

Nancy greeted me with a pleasant smile and led me to the women's lounge where she left me to freshen up. Alone and surrounded by full length mirrors should have been enough to stroke my ego, but the exhibitionist in me would have preferred another warm body to witness my transformation from disenchanted traveler to vivacious mermaid.

I shed my clothing, then paused for a brief moment to admire my naked form in the mirrors. Every inch of my bared flesh tingled with a gleeful anticipation of the days upcoming delights. I reveled in the sensation, while tantalizing myself with the idea of engaging in the frenzied movements of wild sex with Dylan.

With ease I pulled on the vibrant blue suit bottom. A wave of heat surged through my veins as I realized the suit he purchased was a thong with fringe that tickled my ass every time it lightly swayed against my flesh. The suit top left nothing to the imagination, mere diminutive triangles of fabric which barely covered my breasts. I vigilantly tied the gauzy crimson sarong about my waist and then swayed my hips to watch as the ties dangled about my thigh, most alluringly. Once garbed in Dylan's outfit, I pulled a brush from my bag and quickly twined my long locks into two braids; this way the captain's hat would easily rest on my head. I gave myself a final glance in the mirror and giggled, knowing the arousal that this outfit would most assuredly cause.

I exited the women's lounge with a confident flair and an extra swoosh in my stride. I found Nancy standing behind her desk. I walked over to her and she handed me a little map of the docks which showed me exactly where to find Dylan. His boat was moored at the end of the second row, slip D-17. Being perfectly adorned for boating, I took my travel bag in hand and sauntered down the dock anxious for my weekend of wonder to begin.

As I turned down the second row Dylan's handsome form came into view. He wore light khaki shorts and a stark white, skin tight t-shirt. His black hair glistened in the sun, accenting his darkly bronzed skin. I froze, awestruck, unable to move as I eyed his magnificent form. A smile broadened his lips as he began to walk toward me, arms outstretched. When he reached me he took me into a full body contact hug.

"I'm so glad you're here," he whispered into my ear as his hands roamed the bared, warm flesh of my back.

"Me too," I replied. My unspoken thoughts raced and I inhaled deeply, breathing in the slight musk of the outdoors on his skin.

"You ready to come aboard?" he asked.

"I'm always willing and ready to come," I replied.

"I'll keep that in mind."

"You do that," I said smirking.

"Anyone tell you how fabulous you look in that outfit?"

"You're the first."

"Really?"

"Yeah. Honest. Some hunk gave it to me as a gift, but I think I look even better with it off."

"I'm sure a little indecent exposure from an exquisite siren such as yourself wouldn't make waves with Poseidon. Now what do you say we get this party started?"

"Let's go!" I exclaimed in vibrant jubilation.

Dylan wasted no time reaching our destination; the middle of nowhere, with no land in sight. Once he shut the engine off, he disappeared below deck. When he returned, he did so with a bottle of chilled Late Harvest Viognier and a pair of wine glasses which he filled straightaway. Dylan handed one to me, then he lifted his and made a toast, "To the most beautiful first mate ever having set sail with me."

I smiled then lifted my glass to wet my palate.

"Would you like to sunbathe?" he asked.

"Umm not really."

"Would you like to fish?" he inquired.

"No, but I'd love to see your pole," I replied, a devilish grin crossing my lips.

"Thought you'd never ask," he answered, setting his glass on the side rail and moving towards me like a cat getting ready to pounce. He took my glass, set it next to his and gradually pulled the string holding the sarong to my body. The tie gave without effort and the filmy fabric fell to the carpet below.

"Nice," he declared twirling me around to view my scantily clad form. "I just knew you'd look fabulous in blue."

"Uh huh," I murmured.

"Bet you're right about looking better wearing nothing."

"Uh huh," I murmured a little louder.

Wasting no time, Dylan pulled me close and kissed me feverishly on the lips. Lascivious energy flowed from him as he drew my tongue into his mouth and sucked it, soft then hard. Talentedly his kiss began questing a pathway from my lips to my neck. He nibbled on one ear, then the other, and without admonition, he turned me from him and kissed the back of my neck, the heat from his breath bathing me in anguished ecstasy. His hands began to dance rhythmically across my body, caressing my skin lightly, forcing a surge of sexual heat to thrum through me. He untied my top and as it fell to the carpet below he started massaging my breasts. A lustful craving began to flow, lubricating my silken channel for his entrance. "God how I want to feel you deep inside me," I declared.

He didn't reply. Instead, his kisses traveled down my backside and his hands wandered the length of my body until his tongue came to rest upon the top edge of my suit bottom. Ardently, he knelt down and his hands skillfully manipulated the fabric over my hips, down my legs to the floor, where I quickly kicked them aside.

I stood naked. Bared flesh in the middle of a beautifully calm Puget Sound. I leaned forward and rested my arms against the side railing, calculatingly navigating my ass so close to Dylan's face that I could feel his heated breath against my skin.

Instantly he began kissing my exposed flesh, each buttock in turn, and then he temptingly parted my cheeks and teased the taut skin around my anus with his thumbs. The stimulation of his tactical assault forced a shiver to run through my body and in order to quench my newly released hunger I turned and lowered myself to the seat below, halting his advances momentarily.

Newly positioned, I scooted to the edge of the seat and lifted my legs up onto Dylan's broad shoulders, fully exposing my yearning sex to him. He smiled and gave me a quick wink just before his head dropped and his lips found refuge upon the pearly bead of my sex where his tongue traced tiny circles around my clit. His right thumb glided in and out of my alluring softness and his left thumb pressed against the tight sheath of my anus which succumbed willingly to his tender pressure.

"Oh God," I moaned as my body moved to the motion of the sea, back and forth with the gentle rocking of the waves.

The magical sensation Dylan delivered upon my flesh left me pliant and breathless beneath him and as his thumbs pleasured the intimate entrances of my being, my body writhed with reckless abandon. His tongue brushed aginst my clit and I pulled his head in closer to me, unable to bear the exquisite torture he relished upon me. I started to climax.

"Oh God! Ummm. Ohhh. Don't stop! Don't stop! I'm coming! Oh yeah! I'm coming!" My cries echoed across the calm sound as my body shivered in reaction to the explosive starburst swelling within me.

When my breathing began to calm and my eyes opened, I peered down to find Dylan staring back at me, a slightly startled expression beaming across his face. "Wow!" he exclaimed.

"My thoughts exactly," I replied pulling my still quivering legs off his shoulders and pushing myself up to a sitting position. "You don't think we're done, do you?" I questioned as I shakily stood and walked to the back bench seat. "Why don't you come over here and let me show you how we christen a boat where I'm from." I sat down on the cushions below me and waited for Dylan to claim the bountiful prize I offered him.

Dylan stood up and took a bracing gulp of his wine before walking over to stand in front of me. I watched, rapt, as he removed his shirt revealing his chiseled abs. His muscles rippled and the line of his pelvis made my mouth water. I reached out and gently caressed his washboard stomach. His curly dark chest hair accentuated his broad, well defined torso and even the slightest motion of his shoulders caused his pecks to dance for me. Damn, his rock-hard body was unbelievable!

I scooted forward to the edge of the bench, reached out and unbuckled his belt. The outline of his member pulsed as I teased his sex with the tips of my nails through the material of his Khakis. I tore open his shorts, unveiling the stiff up-thrust of his sex.

"Uumm. I love a man who goes Commando."

"Why's that?"

"Let's you know if the guy's the real deal. Much easier to decide if you want to take him home."

"Oh really?"

"Yes. Really."

Hastily, I shimmied his shorts down over his legs, unleashing his burgeoning need. When his prodigious girth came into view, I reached out and began stroking the satin covered steel in front of me. His engorged cock throbbed with every purposeful glide my hand made up and down his shaft. I wantonly leaned forward and licked the tip, tasting the salty essence of his desire. Beneath the masterful advances of my mouth, his body flexed involuntarily.

I wanted to devour him. I aspired to make him feel as wonderful as he'd made me feel. I began to lick the outer length of his dick, from tip to base and then back up again, savoring the warmth of his flesh. As I took his cock fully within the moist, heated confines of my mouth, I reached under his hardened rod and began fondling his balls. His distended flesh pulsed in a rhythmic beat every time my lips maneuvered over the sensitive bulb of his member.

"Enough!" Dylan implored, pulling back from my delectable mouth. "I want to be inside you. I want that pretty pussy of yours to close around me and tempt me. I want to feel your flesh clench, like a vice, hard around my cock. I want to feel the slick warmth of your walls contract against my dick until I can't take it any longer and I come with such force that you'll know you're the vixen you always claimed to be."

I couldn't argue with that. I lay back onto the bench as Dylan knelt down. He took his dick in his hand and rubbed the hardened tip against my clit, just once, then thrust into me with a maddeningly, slow twist. His cock wasn't only long, it was thick, and he filled me with every stroke he made. My sensitive walls stretched with the effort of encompassing him fully within me. My pelvis matched his animalistic hunger and as his pace quickened I grasped his hips and let him lift me in order to bury his girth inside me. I was on the verge of coming when he pulled his rigid cock out of me leaving me awestruck and yearning for more. My ass still writhing beneath him for

"Not yet," he rasped haggardly.

"Oh really?" I replied as I raised my first two fingers to my mouth and licked them; lubricating them in order to begin pleasuring myself by stroking my clit. Dylan's pupils dilated as he watched my fingers play a magical rhythm against my own sex. "I want you inside me while I touch myself, Dylan. Please fuck me," I pleaded.

Dylan obeyed and as his cock once again returned to fuck me, I continued to assuage my clit. Dylan's breathing became ragged and as he thrust inside me I began moaning loudly and without worry for no one was near. My body met his every forceful plunge and together we came with un-restrained passion.

Once our bodies' lust had been quenched, Dylan released me, rose and retrieved two towels which he took to the upper deck where he lay them down. He stood naked in the summer glow and said, "I know you stated that you weren't a salt water swimmer, but I'm going to cool off if you don't mind?"

"Not at all. I'll just lay up here and get tan. Do you have water wings on board in case you need saving?"

"Very funny. Now don't burn that pretty ass of yours before I get back, I have plans for it later."

Once Dylan uttered these words, he dove into the water. I watched in awe as his body became one with the Puget Sound. I was his for as long as he desired. Yesterday he was a sexual daydream. Today, he was all that my fantasies had envisioned: a man, a sea god, my captain! Oh—shiver me timbers!

CHAPTER 18

People might think that having a bottomless bank account equates happiness and wealth means you're going to be happy regardless of the road life takes. I am here to inform you that this is not how it always is.

I have it all: money, beauty, and independence. One morning all this didn't seem to be enough. I had tired of being the woman I pretended to be. I wanted to test my luck in another city, away from my comfortable surroundings. If I found happiness, it would be somewhere other than home.

I traveled for two days, letting the wings of fate guide me. If my scheduled flight deviated, I took the one listed just below it, not caring about the destination. When I finally stopped traveling, I decided to wait until a man approached me.

Believe it or not, only one man was secure enough in himself to breach my self-imposed exile. This is dedicated to that man: the man who rescued me from my subterfuges, the man who was lucky enough to expose the real me.

Destiny's Diversion

I sat, restless in an uncomfortable airport chair, awaiting my fate. The course my life would take seemed unsure, and yet I knew if I waited long enough and listened carefully, my future would show itself.

I closed my eyes while the sounds flowed over me. People scurried past. Some shouted at their partners and kids. Others whispered, just loud enough for me to hear. The sorrowful goodbyes of lovers and the gleeful greetings of missed loved ones coming home. To me they all seemed similar: all planned out and rehearsed. Not once in all the time I was sitting in that chair did I feel that the people around me were really happy and content.

After I'd spent three hours in monotonous waiting and on numerous trips to the lounge, a stranger approached. Instantly, I was drawn to him. His tall, suave, debonair frame seemed to glide across the floor towards me. His head slightly down, his eyes caught mine. The magnetism between us from first glance I knew well, irrefutable lust. His shoulder-length black hair lay in unfettered waves against his cheeks and flowed with his every stride. His blue eyes illuminated his bronze skin. His attire: a perfectly tailored black Armani suit.

To me, the three hours of waiting seemed like nothing compared to the length of time it took for him to finally stand within my reach. My loins awakened as my eyes devoured his captivating good looks. His high broad cheekbones and extremely long black eyelashes hinted at Native American heritage.

I didn't stand until he had extended an open, well-manicured hand to me. "I'm Aaron," he said calmly, with an inviting smile. "And you?"

I took his hand in mine and stood to face him. "My name is whatever you want it to be."

"It's nice to meet you, 'Lady Luck.' You need a ride somewhere?"

"Depends on where you're going."

My hotel. Then dinner. Are you interested?"

"Are you dangerous?" I asked playfully.

"Only if you're looking for a long-term relationship."

"Well, since that's not on my list of wants, or desires,

I'm game. If you're really lucky, I'll even let you kindle my desire."

"Oh my," he replied. "May I take your bag?"

"Yes. Thank you," I answered. I walked with him in silence just staring at him, memorizing the overtly handsome craftsmanship of his entire being.

When we reached the curb outside the airport, I glanced around in search of our transportation. Before I had time to ask, Aaron stated, "My driver's due here momentarily."

I couldn't help but grin. His lips curved up into a half smile every time he spoke. In one way I felt like a hooker waiting for her meal ticket, and in another I felt incredibly lonely and in desperate need of the intimacy of close, personal contact with another human being. Either way, my gut instinct told me that Aaron wasn't a dangerous man. "What is it that you do, Aaron?"

"For a job?"

"Yeah."

"Lawyer. And you?"

"Deserter."

"What do you mean?"

"Umm, I woke up a few days ago and knew I wasn't happy, so I decided to leave my life behind for a while."

"Maybe tonight you can share my happiness with me. After all, you are my 'Lady Luck,' are you not?"

He winked at me, and my thighs tightened with a dreamy desperation. I had been without the smoldering heat of a man's touch for months, yet it felt as though it had been years. I yearned for a man's strength. I wanted to feel the steely hardness of a man's cock pulse against my bare skin. I needed a man to savor my innermost beauty and as I entertained these vivid thoughts my velvet path dampened. The mere idea of experiencing sensational sexual escapades with Aaron unleashed the pent up temptress within me. Even if this was to be a one-night-stand, I hoped we'd skip straight to dessert.

"What are you celebrating?" I asked, seriously intrigued despite my wandering thoughts.

Before he could answer, a shiny black limo pulled up to the curb. The uniformed chauffeur got out, walked around the car and opened the door for us. The driver waited patiently until we both got in, then closed the door behind us.

"What are you celebrating?" I asked again.

"My firm just closed a deal worth millions, 'Lady Luck,' and I'm ready to paint the town."

My eyes cased the limo. Noticing a well-stocked bar I said, "Let's toast to fate's good fortune," and reached for a bottle of champagne.

"Sounds promising."

Aaron took the champagne from my grasp, unintentionally grazing my breasts in the process. My pulse quickened at his touch. I watched hungrily as his strong determined hands twisted the cork, slowly tempting me. I envisioned the seasoned dexterity of his hands teasing my flesh in sweet torment. A feverish warm surge of feminine juices filled me deep into my needy core. My want to throw into the whim of recklessness abandon urged my thirst for sex forward, but both would have to wait until Aaron made the first move. I would be his hostage until then.

The champagne cork exploded, forcing a burst of wet, sticky bubbles to coat my exposed thighs. As the liquid trickled down my calves, Aaron offered, "Let me clean that up for you."

"Don't worry about it," I replied. "Just hand me a paper towel and I'll do the rest."

"You want me to get it wet?"

"Since I'm already wet, I'll just take a glass of bubbly. Then we can get wet together."

His crystal blue eyes were transfixed on mine. He didn't hand me a paper towel, instead he filled my glass flute. I lifted my glass to his and said, "To strangers who open the doors so fate can follow."

"To beautiful women who impair judgment. Although you're a stranger in my car, I can tell you're a dangerously intriguing adversary. I look forward to sparring with you."

"How should our sparring begin?"

He positioned himself on his knees in front of my feet, and then slid off my stilettos. He seemed to know that within his grasp lay a playground of my erogenous zones. He trickled champagne over my painted toes, then paused to take note of my tiny silver toe ring. My eyes drifted shut when his warm tongue began to tease my flesh. He drew my toes into his mouth, one after the other, suckling the tiny digits covered with sweet champagne.

His nimble tongue did not linger long; instead he forged on. His lips nuzzled the arch of my foot, the warmth of his breath against my skin making me shudder with eagerness, and just when I thought I could not stand any more, his teeth gently began to nibble the back of my ankle.

"Round two?" he breathed heatedly.

I was mystified by the sensations rocketing through my body. My eyes fluttered open and caught him in the midst of moving in to take the bottle off the seat.

He grabbed the bottle and playfully held it over my head, laughing as he brought it down again. With a predatory flicker in his eyes, he said, "Turn over and face out the rear window."

After I had positioned myself, I began to unbutton my blouse. I needed to rub my breasts, to assuage the ache of my hardened nipples. He eased my skirt up onto my backside. Wreathed in heat, I pressed my cheek against the soft leather seat. I wanted to fondle his body, to watch his facial expressions as he unleashed himself upon me, but my position made movement impossible. My only choice was to wait, savoring my anticipation.

The shock of cool liquid flowing down between the cheeks of my ass brought me to full attention. Aaron's fingers grasped my hipbones, his lips kissed my tanned buttocks, then his tongue began a fiery trail downward between my cheeks, inching slowly towards the delicate star of my ass. This vortex of feeling elevated me to yet another plateau of pleasure.

My entire being shook as the chilled champagne trickled and Aaron's tongue found refuge pulsing in and out of my most secret, hidden avenue. Skillfully, he parted my legs with a subtle shift of pressure, giving his fingers questing access to my bountiful bed of need. He found the silken flesh of the openly inviting flower of my passion which pulsed under his sensual touch, unrestrained. Tenderly he spread my petals, caressing me in an unspeakably intimate fashion, his lips feverishly sucking in this kinky endeavor.

Desperately, I squeezed my breasts and pinched my nipples, trying to diffuse the bittersweet ache burgeoning between my legs and searing through my ass. My gentle, warm essence flowed onto his eagerly tormenting fingers. Gasping cries caught in my throat when his movements slowed and one of his thick fingers ventured into my velvet path. The heated friction impelled him deeper within me.

The hot scent of sex infused the air, and I became giddy, my strangled gasp echoing in the car. I clenched his fingers within. "Oh God, Aaron, I'm so hot."

Aaron's breathing had become heavy. He tenderly withdrew his hand from my moist cove and caressed my flesh from my belly to the outline of my mouth where he tortured my senses with the heady scent of my feminine desire.

"I want you," he growled lowly into my ear.

I turned over and perched my ass on the seat in front of him, while rapidly shedding the remainder of my clothing. Enthralled, I watched as Aaron let Armani fall by the wayside. His chiseled chest harnessed the iron-hard muscles of his rippled stomach. Tantalizingly, he unzipped his trousers, exposing his unbound length. Then kneeling before me, he waited.

I reached out and took hold of his hard dick. It was silky smooth beneath my touch and pulsed as my hand fondled the length of it. I purred, "I have a grand imagination and the skill of the temptress."

I slid down between his legs so his hands could rest on the seat's edge. I began sucking the tip of his shaft as my hand gripped the hard weight of it and aided its thrust through the tight sheath my hand created. I felt the tip of his cock grow firm and I knew he was close. But before I had a chance to finish him off, he pushed away and took me about the waist, lifting me back into my seat.

Aaron leaned forward and whispered into my ear, "Tonight you will experience total ecstasy within the bounds of *my* imagination. Lay back, I'll do the rest."

My body trembled. His words flowed like an electrical current through my veins. Images of him pleasuring me burnt into my mind. I closed my eyes to experience the bliss he would bestow on me. His masterful tongue parted my mouth; my heart skipped a beat. Our tongues danced in a dueling frenzy, while his hands traced patterns on my naked skin, from the vulnerable curve of my neck down the line of my spine. Passionately he kissed me on the lips as the broad head of his cock nudged against the defenseless portal between my legs.

Aaron's strong hands held me tight as he eased himself deep within my tight coils, using disciplined thrusts that tormented my senses. Clutching his ass, bringing his body close to mine, I matched his every movement in a primitive animalistic dance. He dominated me as he took hold of my hips, lifted my ass off the seat and pulled me over, then leaned back onto the floor of the limo, where he positioned me on top of him. "Ride me," he instructed.

My clit was hard as a rock. As I rode him, I rubbed against his rough pubic hair, bringing myself heightened pleasure. I knew my body. And at any chosen moment I could fulfill my need, but I wanted him to climax with me. I reached behind my ass and caressed his balls as I moved in fluid motion, back and forth. As Aaron neared his peak he dug his nails into the flesh of my ass. Masterfully he maneuvered my body to meet his every unrestrained stroke. I shook in violent ecstasy as my body claimed the last rhythmic contractions from him.

I fell forward, exhausted, and lay on his chest, which rose and fell silently beneath me. Huskily, he whispered into my ear, "Luck was a naughty lady tonight."

I kept my response quiet. Fate had delivered this man to me, and when the cards are placed in front of you, you can't throw them back. I had played the hand life dealt me, and thoroughly enjoyed the ride.

Tomorrow my world may change, yet again, and the hand of fate may toss me another deck of cards, but for now Aaron was my Ace of Spades and he alone could unfold my petals and lead me astray.

1297358